D0099347

A KNIGHT
ON THE TOWN

by

HERMIONE MOON

DEDICATION

To Tony & Chris, my Kiwi boys.

CONTENTS

Catch Up

A Knight on the Town is the second book in The Avalon Café series of cozy witch mysteries that feature me, Gwen Young, and my adventures in the town of Glastonbury, England. Each book features a standalone murder mystery, but my personal story continues through the series. Because of this, if you haven't read it already, you might like to start with *One Dark and Stormy Knight* (Book 1). But here's a short summary of the story if you're beginning here.

All the women in my family are witches. Most of us do spells through our baking, using herbs and ingredients we bless to help people, and I sell my products in The Avalon Café, which is opposite the beautiful Glastonbury Abbey in Somerset, England.

My dad died when I was four, and my mother died six months ago from complications due to Multiple Sclerosis. I'm now twenty-nine. I left university to look after Mum, and I haven't dated anyone since my first boyfriend, Luke, so I've been a little lonely, especially since Mum died.

And then I met Arthur.

Yes, King Arthur—except he insists he wasn't a king. He was a warrior in the sixth century, after the Romans left Britannia, and he led an army that stopped the Saxons invading for many years before he was mortally wounded at the Battle of Camlann.

But he didn't die. His sister, Morgana, also a witch, transferred his soul to a soulstone, a ruby, which ended up in the pommel of a sword, part of a suit of armour that has stood in my café as long as I can remember.

Gradually, Arthur has been waking up, and he insists I'm the reincarnation of his wife, Guinevere, and my dog Merlin is his old friend, the bard Taliesin. I had the ruby set in a gold ring, and yesterday I placed the ring on his finger. He was able to take off the suit of armour, and now he's here, in the tanned and firm flesh. After we solved a murder mystery and put the victim's ghost to rest, I took him home, and here we are, that same evening.

Chapter One

The crystal ball sits on the mantlepiece on a blue ceramic stand.

The ball itself is the size of a bowling ball and completely clear. I polish it several times a week to keep the dust away. In electric light, it has a greenish tinge. In moonlight, it turns silver.

It was my mother's. She would stare at it for hours when I was young, seeing tantalizing glimpses of moments yet to come in the crystal depths.

Most witches practice some method of divination—the telling of the future. I've never been good at it. Nothing spoke to me the way the crystal ball seemed to speak to Mum. Runes stayed as lines on pebbles; the Tarot was just pretty pictures on pieces of card. Lines on a person's palm meant nothing, and tea leaves clung together in clumps. I tried hard with the crystal ball when I was a teenager, but I only ever saw my eyes reflected upside down in the glass, which confused me and made me feel dizzy.

Maybe that's why, when I look into it as I walk past on the way out of the living room, I'm so surprised to see a picture in it that I stand and stare.

Like the way the reflection of my eyes was always upside down, so the picture is upside down, too. I blink several times to focus on it before I realise what it is—a woman, lying down, in a white dress with coloured patches. She reminds me of a painting. It's called *Ophelia* by John Everett Millais. Shakespeare's heroine is singing while floating in a river just before she drowns. The coloured patches on the woman's dress are flowers, the same as on Ophelia's. Her long, light-brown hair is spread out around her head.

Upside down, I can't tell who the woman is. I step closer to peer at her face. But as I move, the picture shifts in the crystal, and it vanishes.

"Gwen?" Behind me, my Aunt Beatrix sounds concerned. "Are you okay?"

I reach out a hand and rest it on top of the ball. The only thing I can see in the crystal now are my upside-down green eyes, intersected by a deep frown line.

"I'm fine." I step away. I must have imagined it. What was I doing? Oh yes, I was on the way to the kitchen.

"She's lost the plot," my Uncle Max says. "Understandable, in the circumstances."

I give him a wry look and open my mouth to reply. My words fade away, however, as someone appears in the doorway.

The sight of King Arthur wearing nothing but a bath towel would make anyone lose the power of speech. Droplets from his dark hair run down his clean-shaven face. He has a slight nick on his jaw where he was obviously getting used to the razor. The white towel circles his waist and hangs to his mid-thigh. His torso is bare, tanned, and muscled.

Merlin, my dog, who's a Labradoodle—a mixture of a Labrador and a Poodle—barks. I think he's laughing.

"Oh," I say, trying not to stare at the way the muscles on Arthur's chest are glistening in the light. "Um, hello."

Arthur meets my eyes, amused, before his gaze slides to the other two people in the room. "Beatrix and Max," he states, holding out his hand. "I'm very pleased to meet you at last."

"Arthur." Beatrix shakes his hand. I can see she's trying not to stare at his chest. "It's so very nice to meet you."

"Please excuse my state of undress." He turns to shake Max's hand. "I hadn't had a bath in fifteen hundred years, so I felt it was only polite to clean myself."

Max laughs and offers him the bag in his other hand. "I brought you some clothes. We're roughly the same build so they should do you for tonight at least."

"Why, thank you." Arthur seems genuinely touched. "That's very thoughtful. I'll go and get dressed."

"I'll make us something to eat," I tell him, conscious that earlier he told me he was ravenous.

"Thank you, Gwen." He smiles and returns up the stairs.

My gaze slides to the others.

"Oh my Goddess," Beatrix says.

I give her a wry look. "Come into the kitchen. I'm going to start dinner."

They follow me into the kitchen and lean against the worktop while I try to concentrate on food. It doesn't work, and I stare at the contents of the fridge for thirty seconds before closing it again. I can't think about anything except the fact that Arthur is here, in my house, and he's real.

"Are you all right?" Beatrix asks. "Do you need to lie down?"

"I do," Max says, making us both laugh. "It's like having a celebrity indoors."

"It's so exciting," Beatrix states.

"He seems very nice," Max says helpfully.

Nice? It occurs to me that although the two of them are keen to help, and I have no doubt that they believe me, they have no real concept of how amazing this is. To them, Arthur is a real person, someone who's turned up on my doorstep, like a long-lost cousin who's visiting from America or the Far East. People's brains are mysterious things, and when we can't figure something out, we often brush over it and accept it at face value. Even Beatrix, who's a witch, is acting like Brad Pitt or George Clooney has come to stay. Not an ancient warrior, who's fought Saxons and killed men with his sword...

"What are you going to cook for him?" Beatrix asks.

"I have no idea." I open the fridge and stare into it again. "What do you cook for someone who hasn't eaten for over a thousand years?"

"Most men like steak," Max says. "I'd start there."

He's probably right. I take out the pack of two eye-fillet steaks. I'll mash some potatoes and do some green beans. Would he like that?

I'm nervous. I want him to feel comfortable and at home, and yet I also want to impress him. I want him to like me. My hands are shaking, and my pulse is racing. I need to calm down or I'm going to have a coronary. And heart attacks definitely aren't sexy.

"There," Arthur states from behind me. "Not too bad at all."

I glance over my shoulder. Max's jogging bottoms hang on Arthur's narrow hips, and they're a little short. The grey T-shirt stretches across his muscular chest, and the sleeves cling to his impressive biceps. But he looks good.

I clear my throat. "I was going to cook you a steak. I'll do it with some mash and green beans, but you can leave whatever you don't like; I won't be offended."

"It all sounds lovely, Gwen. Thank you all for going to such trouble."

"Well, we should go," Beatrix says.

I stare at her in alarm. "Oh. You don't have to…"

She kisses my cheek. "We only came over to bring the clothes and say a quick hello. I'm sure the two of you have a lot to talk about."

Max kisses me too, and they both wave to Arthur before leaving the room. After a few seconds we hear the front door opening and closing, and then we're alone again.

I meet Arthur's blue eyes, and we study each other for a long moment.

"Does my presence in your house make you feel awkward?" he asks.

"No," I lie.

"I understand if it does. Maybe Beatrix has a spare room I could borrow for a night or two until we decide what I'm going to do."

"I don't want you to go." It's the truth. I've been fascinated with this guy since I was a child. I can't believe he's here, in my kitchen, that's all.

His expression softens. "All right," he says.

I turn back to the worktop and pull the bag of potatoes toward me. "Have a seat. Dinner will be a little while."

I meant him to sit at the table in the centre of the room, but instead he pulls up the bar stool I sometimes use when baking and perches beside me. Up close, I can smell the lavender and rosemary from my homemade shower gel he chose from the cabinet. The hair at his temples is a little curly.

I busy myself with peeling the potatoes. Arthur watches me.

"This must be very strange for you," I say. "I mean, it's strange for me, but I can only imagine how you feel, coming to life in the twenty-first century. I think I'd be running around screaming. You seem to be taking it in your stride, though."

"It's maybe not as odd as you'd expect. I've been watching the world for a long time, even if I haven't been fully conscious. I've seen things change. I understand people."

"You must have done, to be able to command an army."

"That was a long time ago," he says.

I chop the peeled potatoes in a colander and then wash them under the tap. "How much do you remember of those days?"

"A little. It's a bit blurry." He watches me tip the potatoes into a saucepan and cover them with water. When I move to put the saucepan on the hob, he leans over and turns the tap on, then off again.

"That's amazing," he says. "No fetching buckets! I like these metal twisty things."

I laugh and switch the hob on. "You mean taps. And you're going to love electricity." I show him how the ring lights up to indicate that it's getting hot and place the saucepan on it.

"Electricity's like magic," he says. "You can't see it, but it's very powerful."

"That's right."

"It could be used for good or evil like magic, too."

"That's true, I suppose. I hadn't thought about it like that." I take some home-grown green beans out of the freezer, put them into a saucepan, and set them to heat. "Life must have been very hard back then."

"We knew no different. It was a lot simpler. People's expectations are very high now. Everyone wants all the amazing inventions. I understand why. But back then life was just about survival."

I open the packet of steak. People would have had to catch the animal they wanted to eat and carve it up themselves. I grow a lot of my own vegetables, but I don't have to grind wheat to make flour. And I'm safe in my little home with its lock and key. I don't have to worry about animals in the woods or invading armies.

I turn and lean against the counter. Arthur bears my scrutiny patiently, as if he understands that even though this is strange for him, it's also a lot for me to take in.

"Am I really the reincarnation of your wife?" I whisper.

"Yes," he says, without hesitation.

"How can you be sure?"

"You'll have to trust me."

"That's a lot to ask."

"I know." He gives a little smile.

"Did we..." I clear my throat. "Did you and Guinevere have children?"

His smile fades. "No. It never happened for us." He looks down at Merlin. I know he can hear Merlin speak, and maybe vice versa. What are they saying to each other?

"How did you release Liza's ghost?" I'm referring to the young woman who was murdered recently, and whose ghost the murderer chained to this spiritual plane with a spell. After I took off his suit of armour, Arthur led me into the library and was able to send Liza's ghost on to wherever we go when we die.

"It wasn't me," he says, "it was Merlin. I just helped a bit."

I look down at the Labradoodle. He licks his nose.

I frown. "I don't understand."

"Morgana gave Taliesin the skill to be able to help those souls who are unable to pass on," Arthur explains. "There are lots of reasons this might happen. Usually it's a very deep grief that binds someone to this plane."

"So he really is psychic," I murmur, bending to ruffle the dog's ears.

"He is. Sometimes, if a person passes in a traumatic way, like murder, they get caught in the memory, reliving the moment over and over. When that happens, Merlin needs a little help. It takes a lot of energy to do what he does."

"And you helped him with Liza?"

"Yes."

"How?"

"By letting him tap into my energy, I think. I've always been strong and healthy." Arthur smiles.

"I suppose if I slept for fifteen hundred years, I might wake up with a bit more oomph." I joke to cover the fact that he does seem extraordinarily well. I have no trouble in believing that this man led an army and fought in battle. There's an… earthiness to him that few men have today.

The potatoes are boiling merrily, so I turn the heat down a little and concentrate on getting out the plates and setting the table.

We haven't yet broached the topic of where we go from here. He hasn't said what he wants to do now he's alive and kicking. He's an intelligent, active man; he's not going to enjoy sitting in the café all day. Will he want to leave Glastonbury? Travel the world?

I feel his gaze on me as I prepare the steaks and begin heating the oil. A few days ago, he told me *I will just have to win you all over again.* Is that still his intention? Or has he changed his mind now he realizes the world is his fresh-and-tasty oyster?

I think about poor dead Liza as I set the steaks to sizzle and drain the potatoes. Liza was married to my first boyfriend, Luke. I loved him once, although any lingering affection I might have felt for him evaporated when I discovered he'd started dating Liza before he and I broke up. But he's the only experience I've ever had of being in love.

We separated a long time ago, around eight years now. I'll be thirty in September. It's still young enough to get married and have children, but I'd begun to wonder if it was in the cards for me.

As I mash the potatoes, my gaze slides to Arthur. He's watching my hands as I add butter and milk, but his gaze lifts to mine as I look at him. His eyes are gentle and warm, and my stomach flutters with butterfly wings. What is he expecting to happen? I feel a little bit panicky. Mum's illness and having to look after her means I've not dated much, and I'm inexperienced in things like this. I look at Merlin, who's studying the two of us. His mouth opens and his tongue lolls out, for all the world as if he's smiling with pleasure. He's glad we're back together. If it's true that I'm Guinevere, then Arthur and I belong together.

Oh Goddess. I'm so nervous! How on earth do I take the first step?

Chapter Two

We sit opposite each other at my pine kitchen table and eat our dinner while Merlin wolfs down his kibble in the corner.

Arthur doesn't start eating immediately, and I realize he's watching me to see what I do—how I handle my knife and fork, how I put salt on, what size bites I take. Of course, in the sixth century he probably wouldn't have used a fork, only a sharp knife to cut off bits of food. I offered him wine and beer, and he chose wine. He has a mouthful of the Merlot and makes a noise that suggests he likes it before he finally has a bite of the steak.

"I'm eating dinner with King Arthur," I say eventually. "This is quite surreal."

He chuckles and scoops up some mash with his fork. "What did you say this was?"

"Potato. It's a root vegetable, originally from America, introduced to Europe in the sixteenth century. You can boil it, mash it, fry it—potatoes are lovely any way they're cooked."

"Do you have a map of the world?" he asks. "I'd like to learn where all these countries are."

"Yes, of course. I'll get you one after dinner." I cut up my steak. It's cooked medium, how I like it. I hope Arthur likes his. He's certainly not complaining as he tucks in. "This must be so daunting for you," I say. "I think I'd be terrified."

"I'm excited." He leans back and has a mouthful of wine. "So many new things to learn."

"Can you…" I hesitate, realizing that what I was about to say might sound insulting.

He raises his eyebrows. "Can I what?"

"Um… I was going to ask if you can read. Modern English, I mean—the language we're speaking."

He tips his head from side to side. "I picked a lot up from the TV. Hopefully you can help with some of the more difficult words."

"Of course."

He meets my gaze and holds it for a moment. "This must be very strange for you," he says softly. "Having a man in your house, when you've lived alone for so long."

I drop my gaze and push a green bean around my plate. "It is a bit odd. Nice, though."

"I'm sure you must be wondering what's going to happen now."

"No," I say brightly. "I wasn't thinking about it at all."

He smiles. "I owe you my life, Gwen. I wouldn't be here if it wasn't for you. I think we should say right now, at the beginning, that you can ask me anything, and that we should talk about everything."

I look back up at him, so pleased he understands. "I'm not very good at this, that's all."

"Me neither."

I give him a wry look. "Oh, I bet you've romanced more than your fair share of ladies."

He gives a short laugh. "Does it help if I say you're the only woman I've ever loved?"

His words take my breath away. I look at Merlin, who's finished his dinner and is now sitting watching us. Then I look back at Arthur. "You mean Guinevere, your wife."

"Well, you're one and the same to me. I've watched you grow from a young girl into a woman. You're gentle and kind, you have a good sense of humour, and a big heart. How could I stand there and watch you day in, day out, and not fall in love with you?"

His eyes are sincere—he means every word he's saying.

"You're talking like I'm a saint," I say, my voice a squeak. "I'm not."

He chuckles. "No, I know. You're grumpy in the mornings before you have your coffee. You lack self-confidence in your personal life and in your witchcraft. You're a bit OCD."

"I'm not!" I pout. "Well, only a little."

"You're also beautiful. You had red hair before, but now it has gold highlights in it. It's much prettier."

Illogically, it pleases me that he prefers my hair to hers. Even though, apparently, we're one and the same person.

I sigh and push away my plate. I suppose there's no sense in skirting around the issues we have to discuss. He's right—we should talk about everything up front. That way we don't have to worry that one of us is thinking something they'd rather not say.

"You're here now," I begin. "Alive, and presumably here to stay. So what do you want to do with your life?"

"I thought I might get a job," he says.

My eyebrows rise. "A job?"

"Your economy is a monetary one. I need to earn a living and pay my way." He cuts another piece of steak. "I'm good with my hands; I can handle wood and metal."

"Uncle Max manages a building company," I say. "I suppose he might be able to find you work."

"He did seem keen to help."

"You don't want to travel?" I ask. "To explore this strange new world? To meet new people and have new experiences?"

"Yes," he says. "With you. But first, we need to get to know each other again, don't we?"

I feel a swell of joy, and nod happily. "Yes, I suppose."

"As I said, if you'd rather I stay somewhere else, I can do that, if you're uncomfortable with me staying here. I don't want you to feel awkward telling other people that you're living with a man."

"I don't care what other people think," I tell him. It's a half-truth. I'm trying to be brave.

He swirls his wine around his glass, his eyes on mine. "Good." He likes me being bold. Oh… this man is going to lead me astray, I can feel it.

"But… I need to go slowly," I say. My face heats a little. How do I explain what's on my mind? "I… um… don't know what you're expecting, but I need time before… you know… we… advance our… relationship…" I stop, feeling as if my tongue is tripping over itself. My cheeks are now burning.

Arthur stares at me. I half expect him to make fun of me, but instead, he frowns. "I might come from the sixth century, but I'm not an animal."

Oh dear, I've insulted him. His expression softens at my obvious alarm, and he reaches out a hand on the table, palm up. I look at it, then shyly slide my hand into his.

He closes his fingers around mine. "I know you don't remember me. We'll take as much time as you need. I just want to be with you, be around you."

I look at his hand, big and strong, and watch as he strokes the back of my fingers with his thumb. "Thank you for understanding," I whisper.

He squeezes my fingers, then releases my hand. "Now, I need to finish this steak. It's amazing."

I laugh and rise to take my plate over to the sink. "I'm glad you like it. What do you want for dessert?"

"Dessert?"

Of course, he would never have tasted sugar; it wasn't used in England until the eleventh century, when it was discovered as a result of the Crusades. He would have had fruit—apples and plums, cherries and berries, but no real desserts as such.

I go over to the fridge, take out a packet, and bring it back. Arthur eyes it as he eats the last mouthful of mashed potato.

"Chocolate," he says.

"Mmm." I begin breaking the bar up into squares. He pushes the plate away, and I open the packet and offer it to him. He takes a piece and examines it, then pops it in his mouth and sucks.

His eyes meet mine, and we both smile.

"I often wondered what all the fuss was about," he says. "Now I know."

"Best thing ever invented," I tell him, eating a piece myself. "But this is just a snack. I'll get you a proper dessert."

I take a chocolate pudding out of the freezer, heat it up, and serve it to him with several scoops of ice cream and chocolate sauce. He eats the lot, scraping the dish afterward until there's hardly anything left on it.

"I'd lick it," he says, "but I have a feeling that's not done in polite society."

I chuckle and place the bowl in the dishwasher. "Not really, no." I close the dishwasher door and switch it on. "Come on, let's go into the living room and I'll get you that map."

I switch on the two lamps in the living room, casting the room in a warm glow. The light warms the crystal ball, turning it into a small sun, and I study it for a moment, wondering whether the picture of the woman in white is going to reappear. It doesn't, though. I glance over my shoulder to see Arthur and Merlin watching me, and give them both an uneasy smile before I retrieve the world map that's rolled up next to the bookcase. After unrolling it, I stick it to the coffee table with a few pieces of Blu-Tack. Arthur sits on the sofa and stares at it, and I sit next to him. Merlin jumps up and puts his front paws on the table so he can see.

"We're here." I tap a finger on the south-west of England, and then point on the map to each place I mention. "This is Europe, and Asia, and Africa. And here, across the Atlantic, is America."

"It's so big." His eyes are wide. "I never knew."

"It took a long time for people to map it all. New Zealand was probably the last piece of land to be found." I show him Australia and the two islands of New Zealand, drifting in the Pacific, and Antarctica, right at the bottom.

"It's amazing." He pores over the map for a long time, asking me to read out the names of some of the places, repeating them after me, and I realize he's learning about the formation of words and letters too, teaching himself how to read.

After this, I show him the bookcases with all the books that Mum and I have collected over the years on a wide variety of topics.

"Tomorrow, I'll show you my iPad," I tease. "It can hold several thousand books."

"Several thousand?"

"I know. Goddess bless the modern world."

He chuckles, running his fingers over the shelf of books. "It's hard to know where to start."

"I have an idea." I extract a slender volume from the bottom shelf, feeling a touch of mischief. I turn it over and show him the title. *The Tales of King Arthur.* His eyebrows rise. "I thought maybe you should know the legend you've become," I tell him softly.

Without saying anything, he takes the book from my hand and goes over to the sofa. I sit beside him, watching as he opens the front cover and studies the drawing on the first page. It's of a handsome knight on a white horse, wearing medieval-style plate armour, the colourful pennant hanging from his lance flying in the breeze.

He turns the page. "Will you read it to me?"

I rest a finger under the words and read him the story.

It begins with Uther Pendragon, who asked Merlin to disguise him as his enemy, Gorlois, so he could sleep with his wife, the lady Igraine. As a price, Merlin asked him for his firstborn child, and when Arthur was born, he came to take him away. The tale continues with the story of how Arthur became king by drawing Excalibur from the stone, and

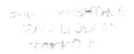

goes on to describe the Knights of the Round Table, the legend of the Holy Grail, and his death on the Isle of Avalon.

When I'm done, Arthur takes the book and reads through it again, studying the pictures. I can't tell what he's thinking, and for a moment I wonder whether I've upset him.

"This isn't me," he says eventually, his fingers lingering on the drawing of him in plate armour.

"I know."

"We didn't have plate armour, only leather and some chain mail. But there are elements of us here." He turns to the page where the king marries Guinevere. "She has red hair." He looks up at me. His eyes are very blue.

I'm still not sure I believe that I was the Guinevere from this picture. It seems incredible, too strange to be true. And yet I do feel that my heart knows him.

"I'm no legendary hero," he says.

I give a little shrug. "You might not be a medieval knight. But you're still a hero, to me, anyway. My knight in shining armour."

He looks back at the picture. "I don't want you to be disappointed in me."

"Arthur, you could never disappoint me."

"Excalibur isn't real. The sword was just a sword."

"I know."

"I wish I could have been a king for you. But I'm just a man."

He's not being coy; his eyes are wistful, his gaze distant. He's sad that the legend is so far from the truth.

"The story is just icing on the cake," I tell him, only then realizing he doesn't know what icing is. "It's like a set of fancy clothes. Beneath them, the man is still the same. Yes, this book tells a fantastical story. But the scholars in this country know the amazing job you did, keeping the Saxons away for so long. I've always been fascinated by you."

His gaze comes back to me, and I blush.

"What would you like to do now?" I ask him. "Watch TV?"

He shakes his head. "Tell me stuff."

"Stuff?"

"Anything you like. I like listening to you talk."

So I pour us another glass of wine, then curl up on the settee beside him. I start with history, picking out major events of the last millennia, trying to give him a flavour of the things that have changed. He stops me often to clarify people and places and to describe developments in technology. He doesn't seem frightened by any of it; he's like a sponge and soaks up everything I say.

The moon rises in the sky and moves across the window as the night grows long. We don't touch. But I'm acutely conscious of him there. And when, sometime later while I'm telling him about the Industrial Revolution, he rests his hand on the sofa cushion, palm up, I don't hesitate to slide mine into it.

Chapter Three

We talk until I can't keep my eyes open any longer, and I declare I have to go to sleep before I fall over. Mum's old room still contains her bed, although I've mostly cleared out her clothes and the rest of her things, so after letting Merlin out for the last time, we go upstairs, and I show Arthur the room.

He lies on top of the bed and tucks his arms under his head. "It's the best bed I've ever had. The pillows are so soft! And this blanket... it's all padded."

"It's called a duvet."

"I love it."

I chuckle. "Goodnight. I hope you sleep well."

"Goodnight, Gwen." He doesn't move, just sends me a smile. "Thank you for everything you've done for me today."

"You're welcome." I hesitate, wanting to tell him how wonderful it is that he's here, but I can't think how to phrase it.

His smile widens a little. "Sleep tight," he says.

I nod and go out. I shut the door behind me and go into my own room, leaving Merlin in the hallway between our two rooms, keeping guard. I get into bed and pull the duvet up to my nose, conscious of Arthur the other side of the wall. He's here; he's really here. I want to lie there and think about him, but I'm worn out by the events of the day, and it's not long before I fall asleep.

I still wake up as usual around six thirty and go out of the room to discover Arthur's room already empty. The bed has been made, guy style, and Merlin's missing too. Downstairs, I can hear Arthur humming, and the distinct sound of milk being steamed in the coffee machine.

Smiling, I take a shower and get ready, then go downstairs. They're in the kitchen, Merlin lying under the table at Arthur's feet. Arthur's wearing a pair of black trousers and a dark grey sweater. He's drinking a latte and reading, although he looks up and smiles as I go in and pushes a mug of coffee across to me. "I've watched you and Cooper make these enough times," he announces. "I thought I'd give it a try."

I pick up the mug and sip it. It's perfect. "What do you think?"

"It's amazing. I love coffee."

I laugh. "I knew you would. Did you sleep at all?"

"I've slept long enough."

"I suppose so." I gesture at the book on the table. "What are you reading?"

He shows me the cover. It's Bill Bryson's *A Short History of Nearly Everything*.

"Starting small?" I say, amused.

"There's so much to learn. It's difficult to know where to start. I'm reading about the solar system at the moment. It's fascinating. Men have been to the moon!"

"It is wonderful, I know."

While I drink my coffee, I make us some toast, and we sit and eat it while he tells me some more about the things he's learned. I love his childlike fascination with science and the world around him. It's refreshing when so many people are dismissive of every marvellous thing they see.

As he finishes the last mouthful of coffee, he looks down at Merlin and studies him for a moment. I have a feeling they're having a conversation.

After a few moments, Arthur gives a little nod and turns his attention back to me. "Can we go out this morning? Around the town?"

"I'm supposed to work," I reply. "But Tuesdays are usually quiet. Let me see what I can do." I take out my mobile and ring Delia. Arthur watches me, puzzled and fascinated by the phone.

"You want a day off?" She sounds most amused. "I can't remember the last time you said that."

"An old friend turned up on my doorstep last night," I tell her, watching him as I speak. He sips his coffee, his eyes twinkling. "I'd like to spend some time with him."

"Him? Gwen!"

I laugh. "Don't get excited. I haven't seen him for a while, that's all."

"Of course, take as long as you need. Melissa's not got much on; she can help out."

Melissa is Delia's sister, and she often works in the café if I need some extra staff.

"Are you sure she'll be all right with the short notice?" I ask.

"She'll be fine. She's bored silly at the moment. Go on, enjoy yourself."

"Thanks, Delia. Speak to you tomorrow."

I turn off my mobile. "All good," I tell him. "I'm free for the day."

"You spoke to Delia through that little black box?"

"Yes. You can talk to anyone you like, if you know the number of their phone."

He nods in wonder. He's finished his coffee, and stands to lean against the counter, his hands in his pockets. "You look like a modern-day man standing like that," I tell him.

"I love pockets," he declares, taking out the pound coin I gave him earlier when I was telling him about the current monarch, and turning it over in his fingers. "You can put things in them! Great idea, and so simple. I don't know why we didn't invent them."

I grin, go out into the hallway, and take my coat from the hook. "How do the shoes fit?"

"They're odd." He looks down at the trainers Max gave him.

"Too tight?"

"No, it's just strange having my feet so enclosed. The leather is very rigid. They're comfortable though."

"Here." I pass him the black jacket that Max included in the bag, and Arthur pulls it on. He surveys the zip suspiciously. I show him how to do it up, and he pulls the tag up and down with surprise, fascinated by the mechanism.

"Amazing," he says.

"You're very easily pleased." I open the door and let Merlin go first, then follow him out. "Come on. Let's stretch our legs."

It rained briefly last night, but today the sun is shining, and the air smells fresh. Arthur seems eager to get out and explore the town, and experience this brave new world.

"Do you want to get some breakfast in a café?" I ask him, knowing the toast wouldn't have filled him up.

"In a bit," he says. "Can we go to the abbey?"

"Of course." I'm surprised. He must have seen it every day out of the window, but he obviously wants to experience it first-hand.

I live about a five-minute drive out of town, but Arthur says he wants to walk, so we leave the car and stroll with Merlin along the streets. For a while we walk quietly. I'm happy enough to just be with him and watch him looking at everything around him as we go. He stares at the cars, the motorbikes, the people and what they're wearing, a mum with her baby in a pushchair, and a man who runs past us, his earbuds in his ears.

"Why's he running?" Arthur asks.

"He's jogging. It's a way to keep fit." I realise the concept would be new to him. "We no longer have to train for battle, and food is plentiful, so it's easy to over-indulge and not exercise enough." I pat my hips ruefully. "The pounds soon mount up."

"There's nothing attractive about hunger and need," he says. "Believe me."

That makes me think about the things he's been through in his lifetime. I know there were famines in the sixth century, and plague. Life must have been hard.

"I've upset you," he says, obviously reading my expression.

"No, not at all. I don't want you to think I'm callous and unthinking, but of course I am, because I have no idea what you've been through, and what life was like when you were young. We have so much nowadays. We have it so easy."

"Different, not easy," he states. "The most we could hope for was to be content—to be warm, dry, comfortable, and safe. Happiness wasn't a factor. And therefore we didn't feel we'd failed when we didn't achieve it."

"I can see you're going to give me more to think about than I'll be giving you," I tell him as we reach the high street.

He smiles and goes to walk into the road, but I grab his hand and hold him back. "We have to wait for the green pedestrian light."

His fingers close around mine, and he doesn't let go while we stand there, waiting for the traffic to stop. I don't complain.

When the light flashes, we walk across the road and circle the building housing the Arthurian Adventure and the museum, heading for the abbey.

"I'll have to take you around the Adventure later," I tease. "You can see how you're the star of the show."

He gives a short laugh, but he doesn't say anything. I can see him looking ahead, toward the ruins of the old abbey. It would have been built after he was taken to Morgana on the Isle of Avalon, when the area was still surrounded by water, but he obviously has memories of the site.

Of course, this is where the graves of King Arthur and Guinevere are supposed to have been. It gives me a funny feeling in my stomach to think that. Is that why he's gone quiet? We cross the car park, Merlin at our heels, and approach the building housing a shop and the entrance to the abbey.

"Hello, Oscar," I say to the elderly man working in the kiosk.

"Morning, Gwen." He smiles at us. "Having a walk around the abbey?"

"Please." I don't bother showing him my membership card as he knows me well, but I slide the cash for Arthur's entrance fee over. "My friend's visiting and wanted to have a look around."

"Beautiful morning for it." Oscar gives us both a ticket, his gaze curious when it settles on Arthur, but he doesn't say anything more, and we leave the building and head toward the remains of the abbey.

"Oh, it's a living history today," I say with pleasure. When the weather starts warming up, guided tours of the abbey are given by people dressed in medieval costume. One woman in a long dress is leading a small group of visitors down the nave.

I start walking toward the main part of the abbey, but Arthur doesn't move. "Let's go there, first," he says, gesturing to the Lady Chapel.

"Okay." Wondering whether he's bothered by the idea of seeing the graves in the nave, I walk beside him as we head toward the smaller building.

Oscar was right; it is a beautiful morning. As we walk, though, an odd frisson of unease prickles down my spine. Something's not right. The place seems unnaturally still. I can't hear any birdsong. I can just about hear the guide talking to the visitors on our right as she walks down the nave, but other than that, it's oddly quiet. Even the sound of the traffic in the distance seems muted.

"Arthur..." I say, not sure how to put it into words.

But he says, "I know." He holds out his hand, and I slip mine into it without being asked. "This way," he says, as Merlin changes angle and heads toward the stairs that lead up to the first floor. There's a viewing platform there that looks down over the rest of the Lady Chapel.

Dogs are supposed to be on leads in the abbey, and Merlin usually stays glued to my side whenever we walk around, but for the first time he runs ahead and disappears up the stairs. Arthur speeds up too, and I have to jog to keep up with his long legs. Heart racing, I run up the stone steps that curve toward the viewing platform. Arthur gets there first, leans on the barrier, and looks down at the central part of the chapel. I can see from his face that he doesn't like what he sees.

I join him at the barrier and look down. And there I see the exact same scene I saw in the crystal ball last night. A woman lies on the grass, on her back, dressed in a white medieval gown, just like the painting of Ophelia. Her eyes are open, unseeing. There's blood beneath her head, as colourful as the cut flowers that lie scattered on her dress and across the grass.

Quite clearly, she's dead.

Chapter Four

"Oh Goddess." My hand comes up to cover my mouth as I stare down at the body of the woman, at her pale face. Her head is at an odd angle. I think she fell from the viewing platform.

My gaze slides to Arthur, whose mouth is set in a thin, firm line. "You knew," I whisper as I lower my hand. "That's why you wanted to come here."

"Merlin knew," he corrects. "Do you know who she is?"

"Her name's Valerie Hopkins-Brown. She's Matthew Hopkins' sister." Matthew is the local journalist, an unpleasant guy who's doing research on witchcraft in the area. He suspects I'm a witch and is determined to prove it. He's the one who had Sir Boss—the suit of armour that Arthur inhabited before I released him—removed to the museum. I dislike him intensely.

"Poor woman," Arthur says in a tone that suggests he's referring more to her being Matthew's sister than to the fact that she's dead.

"I'd better ring Imogen," I tell him, taking out my phone. My best friend is a Detective Chief Inspector at the local police station. She's just finished solving the case of Liza Banks's murder, so she won't be happy to have another unexplained death. Still, it looks as if this one was an accident.

I dial Imogen's mobile number as we descend the steps that will take us to the ground floor.

"DCI Hobbs," Imogen answers within a few rings.

"It's me," I tell her.

"Oh... good morning." Her voice is filled with smiles. "How are you? How's Arthur?"

"Yes, good. Um... I'm really sorry, but I've got another death to report."

"What? Where? Who? How?"

"It's Valerie Hopkins-Brown. She's lying on the floor of the Lady Chapel in the abbey." We reach the bottom of the steps and walk across to the motionless woman. "I think she fell from the viewing platform. It looks as if her neck is broken."

"Oh, no. Gwen, you seem to be making a habit of this. Stay put and don't touch anything," Imogen says. "Try to keep other people away. Is Arthur with you?"

"Yes." He's dropped to his haunches beside the body, but he isn't touching her. A shaft of sunlight falls across them both, like a spotlight on a stage.

"Good. I'll call it in. We'll be there soon."

"Okay, thanks, Immi." I end the call and slide my phone back into the pocket of my jeans.

I walk over to stand beside Arthur. I feel shaky and a little nauseous as I look down at Valerie. "She was nice," I say. "It's such a terrible shame. She must have fallen."

She's wearing a medieval-style long white gown. She was obviously one of the living history tour guides. She has a simple leather belt around her waist, and the brown hair she usually wears in a braid is loose, fanned out around her head, the way it was in the picture in the crystal ball. She's older than me, maybe late thirties or early forties. I know she has a husband and two teenage children. I swallow hard as sorrow rises within me.

Arthur looks up at me. His eyes are very blue in the sunlight. It occurs to me that I'll have to get him a pair of sunglasses. Then I think it's a weird thought to have right at that moment, and I'm probably in shock.

"Have you seen this?" he says.

I look at where he's pointing. The grass beneath our feet is soft, as it's been raining the last few days. Next to Valerie's body, an object is pressed into the earth, as if someone has trodden on it. It's a watch.

"Merlin says it's yours," Arthur states.

I blink. "What?" I drop to my knees and stare at it. It's a Tissot, with a small face, the hours marked by tiny lines rather than numbers or Roman numerals. It has a brown leather strap. About halfway along the bottom half of the strap is a small red mark.

My jaw drops, and my head spins with confusion. "I lost it a few weeks ago," I whisper. "The red mark is paint—I leaned against one of Beatrix's paintings just before I lost it. I kept meaning to clean it off." I glance at my wrist—I'm currently wearing a waterproof watch with a plastic strap that I bought on holiday in Devon for going in the sea. I don't like it as much, and I was planning to get another nicer one from Mackenzie's Jewellery Shop at some point.

"Why is it here?" I ask him.

Arthur purses his lips. "There are a couple of possibilities. Maybe Valerie found it and has been wearing it, and it came off when she fell."

"If that was the case, why is it trodden into the ground? If it fell off her wrist, wouldn't it just be lying on the top of the grass?"

"Yes. The other option is that someone else was here, and either dropped it, or placed it here."

"Someone else?" I stare at him. "You're saying you don't think this was an accident?"

Arthur doesn't reply. Instead, he glances at Merlin.

"What's he saying?" I whisper.

"He says maybe they're trying to implicate you in the murder."

"Me?" My mouth opens, but no words come out. "Why would they do that?"

"I don't know."

"You're wrong. You have to be wrong."

Arthur's frown lifts. "Okay," he says gently. He pushes up to his feet, puts his arm around my waist, and steers me away from the body. I turn and bury my face in his chest, and his arms come up around me.

"Why would anyone want to kill Valerie?" I whisper. "She was nice. I can't imagine she'd done anyone any harm."

"I don't know." He kisses my forehead. "Shall we pick up the watch?" he murmurs, his mouth close to my ear.

I screw up my eyes. "I can't do that. It's evidence."

"You can't. I can."

I move back a little and look up at him. "You'd do that for me?"

His blue eyes stare into mine. "I'd do anything for you."

I look back at his chest, at the black jacket, the zip pulled halfway up. He doesn't understand what it means to interfere with evidence. It doesn't matter that I didn't commit the crime. The presence of the watch will tell Imogen something about what happened here. I can't remove it simply because I'm worried that someone is trying to involve me in Valerie's death.

I rest my cheek on his chest, and his arms tighten around me. It's been a long, long time since I've had a man hold me like this. Luke was never very good at consolation, anyway. He wasn't a cuddly man.

Arthur appears to be a hugger. I like that.

We stand that way for a few minutes, in the warm spring sunshine, while we wait for the police to arrive.

"I saw her," I whisper, enjoying the close contact. "When I looked in the crystal ball last night. I saw Valerie lying there exactly like this, only the picture was upside down and I didn't recognize her."

"Really?"

"I've never been any good at divination before," I tell him. "Why now? Is it because you're here?"

"I don't think so. Maybe you're starting to develop your powers."

I look at Merlin, who's sitting there, watching us. "How did he know to come here?"

"He gets messages from people who are in need of help."

"Dead people?"

"Yes."

"Only I would have a psychic dog," I mumble.

"He's very special," Arthur says, stroking my back. "I think maybe we're here to help him help others."

Merlin's tongue lolls out of his mouth as if he's smiling at me. I give him a little smile back, but it's not easy.

In the distance, the wail of sirens grows louder, and I sigh and withdraw from Arthur. "The police are here."

"Do you want me to go?"

"Of course not. Why would I want that?"

He shrugs. "I don't want you to feel you have to keep explaining my presence here."

"You're my friend," I tell him. "Come to visit. Nobody needs to know anything more than that."

In less than a minute, we're surrounded by uniformed officers and paramedics, who attend to Valerie and quickly confirm that she has indeed passed away.

"Well, well, well," Imogen says, walking over to us. "You could at least have given me one day off."

"I know you get bored." I try to joke, but I'm still shaking a little. She eyes me shrewdly, then turns her attention to the man standing quietly beside me as she strokes Merlin's head.

"Hello, Arthur," she says.

"Good morning, Imogen," he replies.

She grins, showing dimples in her cheeks, taking in his outfit and the way he's standing with his hands in his pockets, but she doesn't say anything more. Her gaze slides back to Valerie, and her smile fades. "What a shame," she says. "I wonder how she fell."

I exchange a glance with Arthur, take a deep breath, and lead her forward to Valerie's body. "I have to show you something." Making sure that I don't interfere with the paramedics, I indicate the watch in the ground. An officer has already discovered it and is bending to examine it. "It's mine," I tell them.

Imogen glances up at me. "You just dropped it?"

"No. It was squished into the mud when we arrived."

She straightens and looks me in the eye. "What are you saying? That Valerie had it, and it came off when she fell?"

"That's one possibility." I rub my nose. "Arthur also suggested that someone else planted it there."

Imogen looks at me for a long time.

"You want to put handcuffs on me?" I ask her.

She gives a small smile. "I don't think that'll be necessary. I do need to take a statement from you, though. Will you come to the station?"

"I'd be happy to." I glance at Arthur. "Can he come with me?"

"Yes, of course, if he wants to."

Arthur's listening to us, and he nods.

"All right," Imogen says. "I'll get someone to take you there. Let me just give a few instructions."

We stand to one side while she explains how she wants the area roped off and secured, and her team begins to follow her directions, ushering away the small crowd that's starting to gather, while the pathologist inspects the body.

"Are you okay?" Arthur asks me.

I nod, even though I'm not. "I don't like the idea that I'm going to be involved with dead people from now on."

"We don't always get to choose what we do in life," he says.

"Do you think that's why all this is happening?" I ask. "Why you've woken up, and Merlin came to me? So we can help people?"

"Yes," Arthur says.

"So I'm, like, going to be busting ghosts from now on?"

"You know who you're gonna call." He gestures to himself and Merlin, and smiles. He was obviously watching when I had the movie on the TV a few weeks back. "Actually it's Merlin who does the busting. We're just his assistants."

I try to laugh, but the scene is too surreal, with poor dead Valerie lying there, her blood soaking into the grass. "So did her ghost talk to Merlin? Does that mean someone's cast The Star Sign Spell on her?" That was how Liza Banks was chained to this plane.

"No," Arthur replies. "Merlin says that when a person passes in a dramatic fashion, sometimes they become encased in the moment of trauma, reliving it over and over again. If a ghost has been here a long time, he's sometimes able to communicate with them. But if they've recently passed, he senses their pain. Unfortunately, he can't ask Valerie what happened. He can just feel her here, imprisoned by the shock of the incident."

"He helps them move on to heaven?"

"He calls it the Summerlands, but yes, in essence that's right. He finds out how they died and helps them come to terms with it. But he says it's been hard on his own, and he's glad we're here to help him."

"I do want to help Valerie," I tell Arthur and Merlin. "I don't like the idea of her being stuck here."

"Did you like her?" Arthur asks. "Even though she was Matthew's sister?"

"They were estranged and never spoke. I'm not sure why. She was nicer than he was, although she could be quite outspoken, too. But she was important in the community—she did a lot at the high school where her children go, and she ran clubs and did charity work. She will be missed." I feel sad at the thought. Imogen will have to tell Bradley, her husband, that she's dead. That's going to be hard.

"I wonder why I saw her death in the crystal ball," I murmur, watching as the police officer finishes taking photographs of my watch, lifts it with a gloved hand, and puts it into a clear plastic bag. I look up at Arthur. "Do you think she was murdered?"

"The barrier from the viewing platform is waist high," he says. "It should stop anyone falling over it. She could have jumped, I suppose. But the presence of the watch..." He frowns.

I look down at Merlin. His big brown eyes study me with concern. He's worried for me, I can tell.

Someone wanted to place me at the scene. I'm sure it was coincidence that I was one of the first people to find Valerie. Thankfully, Imogen won't jump to any conclusions. But it makes me very uneasy to think that someone wants to implicate me in Valerie's death.

Chapter Five

A police officer drives us to the station, and Arthur, Merlin, and I wait for Imogen to arrive.

I worry that Arthur's going to get bored, but I don't think the word is in his vocabulary. He seems to find everything fascinating. He watches the police officers doing their work, and the general public coming and going, and occasionally asks me questions to clarify his understanding.

I'm impressed at how he doesn't seem at all nervous or anxious. I suppose his whole situation is so weird that this is all normal for him. But he doesn't appear worried about making a mistake or saying something wrong in his strange new environment. He takes it all in his stride.

Looking out of the window, I watch the light rain that's started to fall and try not to think about it landing on Valerie's face and dress. I wish I could be as confident and untouched by the world around me as Arthur is. I'm still shaking from the shock of finding Valerie's body. I can't believe I found her, just a week after discovering poor Liza.

I look back at Arthur, expecting to find him watching the scene before him, but instead I find his gaze on me, a frown line between his blue eyes.

"Are you okay?" he says.

I nod, even though I'm not.

"Want a hug?" he asks.

More than anything in the world, I want this man's arms around me, but I'm afraid of seeming too needy. Arthur just smiles, though, obviously seeing it in my eyes, and lifts his arm. I move a little closer to him, and he lowers his arm around my shoulders. He's warm and solid, his touch grounding me. It's only then that I realize I'm terrified he'll vanish, the way he used to when he was in the suit of armour.

"Will you stay?" I whisper.

"I'm not going anywhere," he says.

I swallow and nod, then rest my head on his shoulder, and we sit there like that for a long time, until the doors part and Imogen finally comes into the station.

"I'm so sorry." She walks up to us. Her brown hair in its tight bun is wet and shiny, like glossy melted chocolate. She has dark shadows under her eyes, and she doesn't comment on the fact that Arthur has his arm around me, so I know she's distracted. It was only last night that she brought Mary Paxton in, and I know she would have worked late, interviewing and writing reports. I feel guilty to have brought her a new case, then scold myself. It was hardly my fault.

"Would you like to come through?" Her eyes meet mine then and she gives me a small, mischievous smile, so I know she's spotted our hug, but she doesn't comment on it.

Arthur and I stand and, with Merlin at our heels, we follow Imogen as she punches in a code and goes through the double doors into the main part of the station. She leads us through the busy office to her room at the back, and we sit in the two chairs facing her desk as she takes her seat behind it.

"I'm so sorry to have kept you waiting," she says. "I went to Valerie's home to speak to Bradley." She pulls a face.

"That must have been awful." I can't imagine how terrible it must be to have to tell someone their partner has died.

"She'd only left home about an hour before. He'd just taken the kids to school." She shakes her head. "He called his mother to ask her to pick them up. I could hear her crying over the phone." She sighs and leans on her desk, looking around at the piles of paper and folders littering the surface. "I suppose I'd better start a new set of files."

"I'm so sorry, Immi."

She smiles at me then. "It's hardly your fault." Her gaze slides to Arthur, and her lips curve up a little more. "How are you doing?" she asks softly.

"I'm good, thank you," he says.

"Did you sleep well?"

He gives a small shrug. I have a feeling he didn't sleep at all.

"Okay." Imogen pulls her keyboard toward her. "Bradley's coming in soon to identify her body, so I'd better take your statements."

We tell her what happened this morning—how we decided to walk to the abbey, and what happened when we got to the Lady Chapel and went up the stairs.

"What made you decide to go to the abbey?" she asks. "Why not just walk through the town?"

I glance at Arthur. He doesn't look at me. "That was my fault," he says. "I asked Gwen to take me there. It's a special place for me. I wanted to look around." He doesn't mention Merlin, so I don't either. Imogen is extremely open-minded and seems to believe everything I've told her, but I'm sure even she'd blink at the notion of a psychic dog.

"So you saw Valerie's body from the viewing platform," she continues. "What were your initial thoughts?"

"I assumed she fell," I reply. "Her head was at a strange angle..." I stop and clear my throat. "Anyway, that's what I thought happened. Then we went down to look at her. That's when we found my watch in the grass. It looked as if someone had stood on it and pushed it into the mud."

"You definitely didn't drop it this morning?"

"No. I lost it a few weeks ago."

"And you're sure it was yours?"

"Definitely. It's the same brand, the same strap, and it has a red paint mark on it, from Beatrix's artwork, that I hadn't got around to cleaning off."

Imogen nods, leans an elbow on her desk, and rests her chin on her hand as she studies us. "What do you think it means?" she asks.

"I don't know," I say slowly. "Arthur said Valerie could have been wearing it, and it came off when she fell."

"But someone stood on it," Imogen replies.

"Maybe she rolled on it."

"There's a footprint in the mud," she announces. "Over the watch. We're making a cast of it."

"Oh." I rub my nose. "Then obviously, it implies somebody else was there."

"It doesn't mean foul play," Arthur points out. "The person could have come across her body before us, gone up to have a look, been frightened, and run away."

"Possibly," Imogen says, in a tone that suggests she's convinced that's not the case. "We'll have to have a post-mortem, and we'll see if SOCO comes up with any evidence from the scene." She pulls out her phone, taps a few buttons, then turns it around and offers to me. "What do you make of that?"

I take the phone and show Arthur the screen. He stares at it, fascinated—not so much at the subject of the photo that's on there, I think, but more that the screen has a picture on it.

"The phone has a camera built in," I tell him.

"Amazing," he says.

"I suppose it is," Imogen replies.

I study the photo, conscious of Arthur looking over my shoulder. It's of a tattoo on the underside of a person's wrist. It's obviously Valerie's arm; it's lying on grass, palm up. Imogen must have taken it at the scene. The tattoo is a triangular shape, made of three interlaced arcs. And underneath there are the letters M and S. "It's a triquetra," I say, and hand back the phone.

Imogen frowns. "What's that?"

"It's a design found in architecture, like the Anglo-Saxon frith stool at Hexham Abbey, and illuminated manuscripts like the Book of Kells."

"I've not seen it," Arthur says.

"It dates from about the seventh century, so you wouldn't have."

"What does it mean?" Imogen asks.

I frown, thinking. "It's also found on runestones and early Germanic coins. It sometimes represents the Christian trinity, and it's used in Buddhism, in Japan. It's also found in Celtic knotwork, to represent the Triple Goddess."

"What's the Triple Goddess?" she wants to know.

"In Paganism it's a representation of the three phases of a woman's life—the Maiden, the Mother, and the Crone or Wise Woman. And it also represents the phases of the Moon—waning, full, and waxing."

Imogen taps her pen against her lips as she thinks. "Hmm."

"This was on Valerie's wrist?" I ask.

"Yes."

"What does the M and S relate to?" Arthur asks.

"I don't know," Imogen replies. "Marks and Spencer?"

I stifle a nervous giggle. "I can't imagine she'd have a tattoo of that." I feel a little light-headed. "You definitely think she was murdered?"

She sits up in her chair at that and shuffles her papers around. "It's far too soon to say yet. Let's wait and see what the evidence says."

"Of course." I know her well enough to see that she's embarrassed at speculating in front of Arthur.

We finish off our statements and then stand to leave. She comes around the table to give Merlin a kiss on his nose, laughing as he licks her face.

"Ring me later?" I ask her. "When you get home?"

"Of course. And call me if you think of anything you haven't mentioned."

"I will. See you later, Immi."

Arthur nods at her, and we leave her office and head out. The police officer who drove us here kindly offers to drive us back the ten minutes or so into Glastonbury, and before long we're walking back up the high street.

"I feel awful," I tell Arthur.

"Valerie was a friend of yours," he says, "and she met a violent end. You're in shock."

"You must have seen a lot of death in your time," I say softly. He would have fought in many battles, and of course there would have been no antibiotics in his time, no understanding of germs. If a person received a cut or caught a chill, they could easily die.

"Yes," he replies. "It doesn't get easier, but I suppose it's not quite as shocking when it's part of everyday life."

"I—" Whatever I was going to say vanishes as the door of the building we're passing opens, and Matthew Hopkins comes out.

I stop walking, and my heart bangs against my ribs. Arthur looks at me, then follows my gaze and stops as Matthew sees me.

It's obvious that Matthew has heard about the death of his sister. All colour has drained from his face, and his lips are set in a hard line.

It's the first time I've seen him since he kissed me a few days ago without my permission. I dislike this man intensely, and from the frown on Arthur's face, he feels much the same way, but even so, my upbringing forces me to be polite.

"Matthew," I say, "I'm so sorry about Valerie."

He walks a few steps toward us, his hands buried in the pockets of his jacket, and stops. He looks at Arthur, standing just a foot away. "Who are you?" he demands.

"Arthur," says Arthur.

Matthew waits for more, and when more obviously isn't forthcoming, he turns back to me.

"He's an old friend," I tell him.

"Boyfriend?" he asks.

I'm so embarrassed, heat floods my face. I have no idea what relationship Arthur and I have, so how can I explain it to anyone else, let alone someone like Matthew?

"That's none of your business," I snap, annoyed that he's made me angry.

His cold green eyes narrow. "Imogen told me you found Valerie."

I nod. "I just happened to be at the abbey."

He narrows his eyes. "Really? It's getting to be a bit of a coincidence, isn't it? The bodies are piling up around you."

"I've discovered two, Matthew. I wouldn't exactly say that's piling up."

"In a week?"

He's right, and I don't know what to say to that, so I just glare at him mutely.

"Will you be going to the funeral?" Arthur asks.

Matthew throws him a look. "What's it to you?"

"I just wondered," Arthur says.

"We understood that you hadn't spoken to Valerie in a while," I point out.

"She deserved everything she got." Twin spots of red appear on his cheekbones. "You witches stir up all kinds of ungodly evil and then wonder why bad things happen to you."

You witches? I glance at Arthur, and his eyebrows rise. He caught the reference. So Valerie was a witch? That would explain the tattoo. Or is the journalist just channelling his ancestor, the Witchfinder General, and seeing witchcraft everywhere?

Matthew obviously realizes he's let something slip and fury fills his face. "Stop sticking your nose in where it doesn't belong," he yells, moving toward me.

Arthur steps in front of him, blocking his way. "I don't think you want to do that," he says. His voice is calm, but he's a big guy, and he manages to sound menacing. At his feet, Merlin growls. Matthew glances at him, then back at Arthur. Without another word, he turns and walks away.

Chapter Six

Are you okay?" Arthur asks.

I hold out a hand, surprised to see it shaking. "I'm not normally this much of a wuss," I tell him. "He gets under my skin, though."

"He's a snake," Arthur says, taking my hand in his larger, warmer one. "What can we do to take your mind off it all? Do you want to go home?"

The thought is appealing, but I'm sure I'll just sit there and stew on everything. "No, we should do something together." We're walking up the high street, toward Magdalene Street, and suddenly I have an idea. "How do you fancy going around the Adventure?"

Arthur looks amused. "Really?"

"I think it will be fun. You can see how the legend of King Arthur has evolved over the years." I've read him my childhood book, but the Adventure brings it to life.

"All right," he agrees. So we walk around the building, past the café where we wave to Delia and her sister. The car park opposite has several police cars, and I can see officers coming and going from the Lady Chapel across the lawn. It occurs to me that they might have closed the Adventure, but when we get there it's still open, so they're obviously trying to keep business as usual.

"Stay here," I say to Merlin, who promptly lies down, and Arthur and I go through the double doors into the building.

We find ourselves in the foyer, with Beatrix's mural of King Arthur drawing Excalibur from the stone opposite us. Arthur studies it quietly as I approach the reception desk, where my friend Helen Redford is serving a couple of visitors.

"Gwen!" she says once they've moved on. "Good morning. Terrible news about Valerie, isn't it?"

"Awful."

"Nathan said you found her body."

I nod, trying not to think about poor, pale Valerie lying on the grass. "It was awful."

"And after Liza, too. How terrible for you."

"I'm beginning to think I'm a jinx," I tell her. "You'd better stop hanging out with me."

She gives a nervous giggle, then puts her fingers over her mouth. "Don't make me laugh. It's not funny."

"No, it's really not." I think of Matthew's words: *It's getting to be a bit of a coincidence, isn't it?* But two incidents *are* a coincidence. It takes three to make a trend.

Helen's gaze slides to Arthur, who's gone over to study the mural close up. "Who's Mr. Gorgeous?" she whispers.

"An old friend, come to visit," I advise. "Funnily enough, his name's Arthur."

"Of course it is," she says. "Wow, Gwen. He's perfect. Are you and he… you know…?"

"Not yet." I give her a wry look as she grins.

"Well if you decide you're not interested, let the rest of us know, won't you?"

Hoping Arthur can't hear us, I glance over at him. He's watching me, and there's a little smile on his face. Oh, he can definitely hear us.

Mumbling under my breath, I pay for the two of us, and Helen gives us our tickets. "Have fun," she says.

I stick my tongue out at her, and she laughs.

"Come on," I tell Arthur, gesturing toward the gate. "This way."

We go through a small gate onto the platform, and wait with Gaby, the assistant, until the next carriage stops on the narrow tracks. She opens the carriage door, and I climb in and settle myself on the cushion. Arthur then gets in beside me, and Gaby lowers the metal bar that locks us in.

The carriages are large enough for three people, but Arthur's a big guy, and he obviously has no intention of keeping his distance from me. He holds out his hand again, and I slip mine into it as the carriage shudders, then sets off on its journey. When it gets to the end of the room, the curtains part, and we enter the first section of the Adventure.

The carriage moves slowly through the displays on either side that tell the story of King Arthur's birth. It's the same as in the book: Uther Pendragon desired Igraine, the wife of Gorlois, and asked Merlin to cast a spell to make him look like Gorlois. In return, Merlin asked for the child of their union.

"Pure fantasy," Arthur says, as we pass a model of a grey-haired Merlin in the process of casting a spell with his wand.

"Who was your father?" I ask.

"His name was Ambrosius Aurelianus. He was the descendant of a Roman provincial governor, and when the Romans left Britain, he was determined not to let the country fall to the invaders." Arthur's eyes are distant, lost in another time. "He brought me up to be a warrior, and to use Roman military methods to defend our shores. He was a great man."

I don't say anything as the curtains part for the carriage to allow it to enter the next room. Here King Arthur is shown drawing the sword Excalibur from the stone.

"That's a typo," Arthur says.

"What?"

He points to the words painted above the scene. "*Arthur gladium ex saxo eripuit. Ex saxo* means 'from the stone.' *Ex Saxon* means 'from a Saxon.' I fought and killed one of the Saxon leaders and took his sword. One of the monks who wrote about the event must have missed off the 'n'."

"Are you serious?"

"It's an easy mistake to make. Funny to think it's spawned a whole legend that never existed."

I'm so astounded, I can only sit with an open mouth as we watch the video behind the models of the young warrior as he pulls out the sword from the stone and is declared king. My gaze slides to Arthur, who's watching the scene, the images reflected in his blue eyes. *I fought and killed one of the Saxon leaders and took his sword.* He's probably killed many men in battle. I'm not sure how I feel about that. But I suppose it's no different to modern-day soldiers who fight to defend their country.

He looks down at me. "Want to feel my muscles?"

That makes me laugh. "Do you have strong memories of the time?"

"No. It's like an old movie I watched many, many years ago. As if it happened to someone else." He looks ahead as the curtains part again, and we enter a larger room that depicts a meal in Camelot, with the Knights of the Round Table.

His fingers thread through mine as we pass slowly through. It's a beautiful display, full of colour and light, the walls painted to make it look as if we're in Camelot, with banners above our heads, and tables filled with food for a feast. We listen to the narrator telling us about the knights and their stories—Sir Gawain and the Green Knight, Sir Tristan and Iseult, Sir Galahad and the Holy Grail, and of course, Sir Lancelot and his love affair with Arthur's queen, Guinevere.

Arthur is silent as we approach the models of the king and queen getting married. Lancelot stands behind them, unsmiling, his jealousy obvious. Arthur told me there was no truth in the story, and I can see from the narrowing of his eyes that he's annoyed.

"I'm sorry," I murmur as the carriage rolls past.

His blue eyes focus on me. "It upsets me that the legend says we were not faithful to one another."

"I know." Behind him, the scene changes to a video of Lancelot leading Guinevere to bed, and her staring up at him lovingly. Arthur doesn't look at it, but keeps his eyes on mine, and suddenly I can't look away. My breath catches in my throat, and my heart bangs against my ribs.

"I never looked at another woman from the moment I laid eyes on you," he says.

I'm so unused to declarations like this that I can't think of anything to say. Luckily, I don't have to.

Arthur's arm lies along the back of the carriage. I'm close to his chest, and I almost fit under his arm. I'm fairly tall for a woman at five-nine, but he feels so much bigger than me.

I lean against him, and he lowers his arm around me, and we sit like that for the rest of the journey.

It's hard to concentrate, but I do my best as we trundle through the story of the Holy Grail. When he helped Merlin send Liza's soul on to the Summerlands, as he called it, he told me that the Grail was a well of energy. It makes sense to me now, that Morgana taught Merlin to draw from the well in order to summon enough power to break the bonds that hold a spirit to this plane. I think about the picture I saw in the crystal ball this morning and wonder whether I would also be able to access the Grail to help with my magic. I've never thought about it like that before. That it could be *real* magic. But I'm beginning to realize there could be more to it than blessing herbs for my baking.

Finally, we come to the last room, which tells about Arthur's death at the Battle of Camlann, and the transportation of his body to the Isle of Avalon. Arthur is silent through this section, and I wonder whether this is the closest the story has come to touching on the truth. I know his men took him to Morgana, and that this was where she cast the spell on him and transferred his soul to the ruby. I glance at the ring on his right hand. It almost feels like a dream now, seeing his eyes in the helm of the suit of armour, and helping him unstrap the plates to set him free.

I look back at the scene. It depicts King Arthur's son, Mordred, thrusting a spear through his father on the battlefield.

"So Mordred wasn't real?" I ask Arthur.

"No. I had no children. I was mortally wounded by an unnamed Saxon who swung an axe that lodged in my neck…" He lifts a hand to rub it, as if he can still feel the blade lodged in the bone.

"Would you like to have children?" I want to distract him from any memory he has of the end, of the pain and unhappiness he must have felt as he lay there and said goodbye to the woman he loved. Guinevere bends over his body, her long red hair—so like mine—spilling onto the ground. It gives me a funny feeling in my stomach.

"If the gods will it," he says. He smiles.

"Were you a Christian?" I ask, conscious that Christianity had reached the shore of Britain by that point.

"I knew of the Christian stories," he says. "But I'm not a scholar or a philosopher. Back then, we had a closer connection with the land. I could feel the turn of the seasons in my blood, and I knew whether it would be a good or bad harvest before the wheat began to ripen. We built our houses and grew our food, and defended our land against those who wanted to come and take it for themselves. We believed there were spirits in the springs, in the earth, in the sun and the stars. The Goddess was the lifeforce that made things grow. The Oak King ruled one half of the year and the Holly King the other. That's all we knew. We left the rest to the monks and the druids."

His low, deep voice mesmerizes me, creating a vision of wheat rippling in the wind, apples ripening on the trees, and the smell of bread baking in the oven. I appreciate technology and medicine and everything that modern times has given me, but part of me yearns for that simpler life.

"I want to feel that connection with the land," I tell him. "At times I'm close to it, when I'm in my garden, and when I'm baking, or celebrating a festival. But it always feels out of reach. Will you... will you teach me?"

"You already have that connection," he says. "And I'm no expert. But I'll help if I can."

Chapter Seven

We emerge through the curtains into the interactive museum, and it's time to disembark. I miss the warmth of his body pressed against mine, as he wanders around, looking at the exhibits. He smiles at the children pressing buttons and trying on pieces of armour, then stands in front of Sir Boss and stares. I walk up to stand beside him.

"Are you okay?" I ask softly.

"It's weird," he says. "I spent so long looking at the world through the slit in this visor. Years and years... I miss him, a bit."

"I can't imagine how strange it must feel." Shyly, I slip my hand into his.

He looks down at it. "I'm sorry if my feelings for you are overwhelming. But I waited so long for you to come back. I mean, I wasn't standing there for all those years waiting, but I was aware of time passing."

"When did you first become more conscious?"

"Around the time of Josephine," he says, naming my great-great-grandmother. "I used to watch her kneading dough in the bakery."

I realise he's talking about the Avalon Café. I'd read somewhere that it used to be a bakery, but his words confirm it.

"What was she like?" I ask as we wander along the line of cabinets that display items supposedly from the 'real' Arthur's time.

"She had red hair, like you." He smiles. "All the women in your family did. Harriet, Lizzie, and your mother, Alice, of course. I've watched you all, in a kind of dream state, I suppose. But it's only been since you were born that I've fully awoken. That's how I knew it was you."

He stops and stares into one of the cabinets. Bending, he peers at an item in the middle. Then he laughs. "That's mine."

"What?" I bend beside him and follow his finger as he rests it on the glass above the object. I studied these in my first year at university.

It's called a zoomorphic penannular brooch—basically, a bronze brooch in the shape of an animal, in this case a bear. Of course—the name Arthur is derived from Arth, the Welsh for bear. He probably wore it on a cloak. It's set with about a dozen small gems, although the one that would mark the bear's eye is missing.

"You gave it to me," he says. "I'd only had it a few weeks when the eye stone vanished. You scolded me for that." He smiles.

My jaw drops. "I gave it to you?"

"On the fifth year of our marriage."

It was an anniversary present? I stare at the item, stunned to see a real piece of our history in the flesh, so to speak. "How long were we married?"

"Eleven years."

I look up at him, shocked into silence. I know the artefacts in this room are from the Dark Age period, found or excavated at dig sites around Glastonbury, but I'd assumed they were examples of objects from the sixth century—illustrations of the life Arthur might have lived. I'd never considered something here might actually belong to him.

And I certainly never thought I might have given it to him.

His blue eyes are warm, amused. "Yes," he teases, "you put up with me for eleven years. Does that surprise you?"

I hold his gaze, knowing as I do that deep inside, I'm beginning to remember the way I felt about him. "No. I'm not surprised at all."

His smile spreads, and for a moment I think he's going to kiss me. But he sighs, stares at the brooch for a bit longer, then continues on.

I pause and rest my fingers on the glass above the brooch. I wish I could get it for him, but of course it's a museum piece, and it needs to be here so everyone can see it and appreciate it.

We walk around the rest of the exhibition, and then we make our way outdoors, into the spring day. Arthur announces he's hungry, so we circle the building, give Merlin a bit of fuss, then leave him outside and go into the Avalon Café. I was going to have to introduce Arthur to the others at some point, so I might as well get it over with.

"Arthur is an old friend who's come to stay for a while," I tell everyone as we approach the counter.

"Hello, Arthur." Delia shakes his hand, her eyes wide. Her gaze slides to mine, bright with amusement, as he shakes hands with Melissa, her sister, who's a couple of years younger than Delia, and a couple of pounds lighter, but otherwise a carbon copy of her sister. "How come you never mentioned him before?" Delia scolds.

"I haven't seen him for a long time," I explain, "and he lives a long way away, so I never thought he'd visit."

Cooper, the young barista who works for me when he's not at college, comes forward. "Hey," Cooper says, "good to meet you."

"You, too." Arthur shakes his hand. Did they do that in the sixth century? I would imagine they would have clasped arms like Russell Crowe did with soldiers in Gladiator, but he's obviously seen others do it.

"Where are you from, then?" Cooper asks.

"New Zealand," Arthur replies without batting an eyelid, obviously recalling the map we studied last night.

"Wow," Delia says, "you have come a long way. Are you enjoying your stay?"

"I'm having a fantastic time," Arthur says. "Apart from the murder, obviously."

Everyone's smile fades, and Delia shakes her head. "I know, awful isn't it? And someone said you found Valerie's body, Gwen."

"Yes, Arthur and I were out walking. It was pure coincidence." I nod as Cooper gestures at the coffee sign, and I put up two fingers, indicating Arthur. "I can't believe it, after what happened to Liza."

"I thought you said you lived in a quiet town where nothing ever happened," Arthur says.

"I got that wrong, didn't I?" I point to the cabinet that holds our hot food, and the one beside it with all the bread, sandwiches, and cakes. "What would you like for lunch?"

"You choose for me."

I order him a roast beef roll and myself a chicken sandwich, and add a couple of pieces of the chocolate cake I made yesterday. Then we take a seat in the window, down from where Merlin's lying in the sun. We take off our jackets and put them over the backs of our chairs.

"New Zealand?" I murmur, smiling.

He laughs. "First thing that came to mind. It sounds like a nice place, anyway. We'll have to go there someday."

I study him, admiring the way his sweater stretches across his impressive chest and arms. We need to get him some more clothes. It'll be interesting to see what kind of things he chooses.

"Would you like to travel?" I ask him.

"Definitely."

"Where do you want to go?"

"Everywhere," he states. "Eventually. But there's no rush. It would be nice to see some of England first."

I think about his statement, There's no rush. I hope he's right. At the moment, I can't shake the feeling that he's going to vanish at some point, but I suppose that's natural considering the situation.

"I'm not going anywhere," he says gently.

I look into his eyes. "Can you be sure about that?"

"Yes," he says. "I can't explain how." He reaches out and picks up my hand where it's lying on the table. "I know it's a lot to ask you to trust me. I am aware of that."

It is a lot to ask, but I understand that he can't prove he's here to stay, so I just smile and shiver inwardly as he brushes his thumb across my fingers.

Cooper delivers our coffees, and I glare at him as he grins at me and flicks his eyebrows up at the sight of us holding hands. "Go away," I tell him, and he laughs and walks off as Arthur chuckles and retrieves his hand.

Melissa delivers our lunch, and we eat while we talk about places we'd like to go and see. After we've finished, we say goodbye to everyone and leave the café, and this time, with Merlin, we head south, to Abbey Park. It's quiet at this time of day. The grass is covered in daisies, and although the air is fresh, there's a feeling that summer isn't too far away.

I have a ball in my pocket, and Arthur throws it for Merlin, while we walk slowly across the grass. "I wonder how Imogen's doing," I say. "She works so hard. I feel guilty for discovering a new case for her."

"It hasn't given her much time to go out with Christian." Arthur names the exhibitions director from the museum that Imogen has a crush on. "Maybe we should see if they want to go out for dinner with us."

I look up at him in delight. "Really?"

"I don't see why not."

"I'd love that. I've never done it. Luke and I were very young when we dated, and although we went out sometimes, it was always in a group, you know? Never with another couple." A woman is walking toward us, head down, lost in thought. A Cocker Spaniel trots, subdued, at her heels. I frown, sure I recognise both the woman and the dog.

"Then we should definitely do it," Arthur replies. "It would be fun. I like Immi, and I'd like to meet Christian properly." He would have seen him come into the café occasionally, but he's not spoken to him yet.

"Yes, I…" My words trail off as the woman lifts her head and looks at us. She's in her mid-forties, on the plump side, wearing jeans and a rather shapeless black jacket. Her dark hair is sprinkled with grey, and looks uncombed. It's Kianna Brown; she's Valerie's sister-in-law. I remember then; the dog is Valerie's.

I stop walking as she reaches us, and she stops too. "Gwen," she says. "Hello."

"Kianna," I reply. "I'm so terribly sorry." I glance at Arthur. "This is Valerie's sister-in-law, and this is Valerie's dog, Beauty. Kianna, this is my friend, Arthur."

"Hello," Arthur says. "I'm very sorry about your sister."

She shakes her head, her eyes glistening. "I still can't believe it. Bradley rang and told me this morning—I'd only just got up. I went straight round. Our parents are there with Valerie's, and her kids. Everyone's just crying all the time. I had to get out of the house, so I said I'd give Beauty a walk." She gives a shadow of a smile at the little dog.

"It's just awful," I reply.

She rubs her nose. "Bradley said you found Valerie."

I stuff my hands in the pocket of my jacket, feeling awkward at the thought. "Yes. I was showing Arthur around the abbey. We just happened to be the first on the scene."

"How terrible for you. But I'm glad it was you and not somebody else less… responsible."

I nod, touched by her words.

"There's going to be an investigation," Kianna says. "Apparently DCI Hobbs told Bradley that it's not clear whether Valerie fell or jumped."

She doesn't mention the possibility that Valerie could have been pushed. I glance at Arthur, who raises an eyebrow. Imogen obviously doesn't want to raise that option unless she has proof.

"It looks as if Beauty would like to have a run with Merlin." Arthur watches the Spaniel and the Labradoodle touching noses as their tails wag.

"Oh, of course." Kianna bends and takes Beauty off the leash. She and I watch as Arthur draws back his arm and throws the ball. It's such an innocuous action, but a little tingle descends my spine. Women don't throw a ball the same way as a man. As both dogs go tearing off over the grass to try to get to it first, it occurs to me that it's been a long time since I've had the company of a man like this, since I've been able to turn to someone for support.

And then I think of Bradley, who's lost his partner in life, and I feel a swell of guilt and sorrow, and a touch of panic. If you don't have anything, then you also have nothing to lose. All love involves an element of risk. Arthur insisted he's here to stay, but I can't be sure of that. What if I fall for him and then one day I wake up and he's no longer there? I know being with him will be wonderful, but do I want to take that kind of risk?

Chapter Eight

I can't think about that now, though—not with Valerie's sister-in-law standing before me, clearly needing to talk.

"How had Valerie been lately?" I ask. I knew her to say hello to, and we'd chat briefly if she came into the café, but that was about it. She was older than I, and we didn't mix in the same circles.

Kianna watches as Arthur bends and takes the ball from Beauty as she returns with it, then throws it again. "Actually, she hadn't been that well," she admits.

"Oh, really?"

"DCI Hobbs asked if Valerie had been depressed, and Bradley had to say yes. She hadn't been herself at all. She was usually so bright and bubbly, but lately she'd been feeling unwell, and I think that influenced her mood."

"Unwell in what way?"

"She was having headaches and feeling dizzy. She had pains in her chest, and she felt confused a lot."

I'm starting to get a prickle up my spine, and I note that when Merlin returns from his run, he stands listening to Kianna, his tongue lolling out as he regains his breath.

"So... do you think she was depressed enough to take her own life?" I ask.

"I don't know. She was going to be forty next week. She joked about getting old, but maybe it had more of an impact than we all realized." Kianna bends to pat Beauty as she runs up to her. "I loved Valerie, but I wasn't as close to her as some of her friends. She met up with them a couple of days ago at the Lady of the Lake for lunch to plan her birthday party."

"Oh, who were her friends?" I ask.

"Fenella Davies is the only one I know," she admits. "She runs Dogs All Day out on The Roman Way."

I've heard of the dog kennels. I'd planned to pay a trip there to check it out sometime in case I wanted to go on holiday and leave Merlin there for a few days. I don't know Fenella, though.

She bends and puts Beauty's leash back on. "Well, I'd better go."

"Of course. Do you know when the funeral is?"

"No, not yet. Probably next week." She straightens. "It's going to be difficult. Obviously, all funerals are difficult, but you know Matthew…" Her lips twist.

"Yes, I know he and Valerie were estranged." I'm loath to probe too deeply and upset her, but equally she was the one who brought it up, and I really want to know what he meant with his comment, *You witches stir up all kinds of ungodly evil and then wonder why bad things happen to you.* "I know Matthew is quite religious," I say carefully. "Is that why he disapproved of Valerie?"

Kianna gives a short, harsh laugh. "He's convinced she's into devil worship or something equally as mad."

"Really?" I make sure my expression mirrors her disbelief. "How odd."

"He's unhinged," Kianna says. She tugs Beauty's leash. "Come on then, poppet. I suppose we'd better get you back and see if there's anything we can do at home."

She walks away, her boots crushing the damp grass into dark prints.

I look at Arthur. "Interesting," he says, as we turn and start walking toward the road.

"I wonder what made Matthew think that Valerie was into devil worship," I say. "He said 'You witches.' Do you think he had proof that she was a practising witch other than what her tattoo implied?"

"Possibly," Arthur replies.

"I wonder if Fenella Davies can tell us anything else."

"Do you want to go and talk to her?"

I chew my bottom lip. "I suppose I should leave it up to Immi. I don't want to interfere in the investigation."

"I don't see how you'd be interfering. You might uncover something useful for her."

"I suppose so, especially with you and Merlin and your sixth senses." I smile at him. "Would you come with me? To see Fenella, I mean? Or is that a little dull for your first day out on the town in the twenty-first century?"

He laughs. "I just want to be with you. I don't mind what we do."

"Okay then," I say happily. "Let's go and pretend to check out the kennels, and we'll see what we can find out."

We walk leisurely back to the house, enjoying the warmth of the spring afternoon. Arthur asks lots of questions as we go—eclectic questions, about the trees and flowers we pass, how a car works, what a lamppost is, how the banking system works… anything that jumps into his mind. I answer as best I can. My general knowledge is average, but I hope I can give him enough of a clue, and he can always look up more details later.

That makes me think of something, and when we get to the house, I ferret around in the bottom drawer in the kitchen and retrieve the item I was looking for.

"It's a spare phone," I tell him. "It works perfectly well. I got myself a new one a month ago as a treat." After Mum died and I sorted out all her finances, I discovered she had a small rainy-day savings fund that I'm pretty sure she was keeping for me. I haven't yet decided what to do with it, but I did give in to temptation and buy a new smartphone.

"I don't think anyone will be calling me," Arthur says, amused.

"It's not only for making calls. You can take photos and record anything you see while you're out and about. And it also connects to the internet, which means you can look up anything you want at any time. Well, providing the phone has a signal." I power the phone up and discover it has a small amount of charge in it. "We can charge it in the car," I tell him. I quickly make him an account, put my credit card on it, and set up a plan that gives him plenty of data, because I have a feeling Mr. Encyclopaedia is going to want to use it a lot.

Then I hand him the phone. I show him how to swipe the screen, and how to access the camera and take a photo. He takes one of me and Merlin, and I show him how to set it as his wallpaper, which he loves. Then I demonstrate how to use the internet.

"It's like a huge library," I explain. "You can type anything into the search engine, and it will give you information on it. Have a go."

He stares at the tiny keyboard on the phone. "The letters are all over the place."

"It's called a QWERTY keyboard—the letters were originally arranged that way for old mechanical typewriters, so the keys didn't jam. You'll soon get used to it. Try typing something."

I wait for him to Google himself or something to do with his past. Instead, his big fingers carefully pressing the letters, he types in 'muffin'.

"Muffin?" I ask with a grin.

"It was the first thing that came to mind," he declares.

"They say men only ever have one of three things on their minds," I tell him. When he raises his eyebrows, I add, "Food, sport, or… something else."

He gives me a mischievous smile. "I don't know about sport, but the other two are probably right."

Chuckling, I point to the phone. "What does it say about muffins?"

He reads the screen. "Apparently it refers to either a part-raised flatbread or a cupcake-like quickbread. That's a bit of a mouthful."

"You can see how it works, though."

"Absolutely. It's amazing." He shakes his head in wonder. "Can I keep this for a while?"

"It's yours," I tell him. "Now come on. Let's go and visit Fenella and see what she has to say."

While I drive to Dogs All Day, Arthur spends his time either staring out of the window or Googling stuff.

"Can I learn to drive?" he asks, watching me navigate a roundabout.

"Of course." I signal to take the second turnoff. "You'll need to learn the Highway Code and have lessons in the car, but I can teach you for a while, when you get your provisional licence. Hmm. You're going to need a birth certificate and a passport. That might be tricky. We'll have to think about that."

He studies the road signs. "The Roman Way. Why's it called that?"

"It will probably be an old Roman road. There are lots of them still."

"I'm not surprised," he says. "The Romans were incredibly innovative. Their knowledge far surpassed the Britons'."

"It's weird to think that for you, the Romans were a hundred or so years ago, like World War One is to us."

"I suppose so." He thinks about that. "We were adamant that we wouldn't lose the technology and civilised way of life they brought us. But it crumbled quickly, didn't it?"

I nod. "Within a couple of hundred years, the Roman cities were deserted. But there are lots of remains still standing. I'll take you to some one day."

I indicate as the sign for Dogs All Day appears to my left, and slow to turn onto the drive. Although houses line the road, behind them, fields dotted with trees lead to the River Brue that winds down to Pomparles Bridge. The drive leading to the kennels passes through two lines of beech trees and finishes at a large country manor house flanked by a series of smaller buildings which are obviously the kennels.

Arthur and I get out of the car, and I open the passenger door and bend down to talk to Merlin. "I'm really sorry about this," I tell the Labradoodle, who eyes the leash in my hand suspiciously. "But we're undercover. Either you go on the leash, or I have to leave you in the car."

Merlin looks up at Arthur. "He'll go on the leash," Arthur translates. "But don't expect him to be happy about it."

"Don't sulk," I tell the dog, clipping it on. "I promise I'll take it off as soon as we get back to the car."

We walk along the flagstone path, and as we approach the kennels, a spate of barking draws out a tall man in his forties, dressed in corduroy trousers and a sweater that's the same shade as his grey hair. He's obviously been working with the dogs, but his Barbour wax jacket and Wellingtons give him the look of an English country gentleman out with the hounds.

"Hi," he says. "Can I help you?"

"We came to have a look at the kennels," I reply. "We're thinking of putting our dog here when we go on holiday in August."

It occurs to me that I'm talking as if Arthur and I are a couple, and I give him a sidelong glance. He just smiles. I suppose he didn't have holidays in the sixth century. I can't imagine a crowd of Romano-British warriors traipsing off to the beach for a paddle.

"Of course," the man says. "I'm Dylan Davies, and I run the kennels with my wife, Fenella. She's the one who does all the bookings. I'll have to see if she's available. She had some rather bad news this morning."

"Oh…" I say, adopting a pained expression, "she wasn't friends with Valerie Hopkins-Brown…"

His eyebrows rise. "Yes, that's right. Did you know her?"

"Sort of… We're the ones who found her this morning."

His mouth forms an O, and he stares at us for a moment before saying, "Fenella is definitely going to want to talk to you. Let me see how she's doing."

We watch him walk away. Arthur looks down at Merlin. "Do you want to go and play with the other dogs?" Merlin barks, and Arthur laughs. "I'm not repeating that."

"I thought you played quite nicely with Beauty this morning," I scold.

"He's embarrassed about that," Arthur says. "He doesn't like admitting he enjoys doing dog things."

I smile, but I'm distracted by Dylan returning down the path with his wife. I feel a twinge of guilt. Fenella was a good friend of Valerie's, and I'm intruding on her grief by being here. But if I manage to find out something that Imogen didn't, surely it will have been worth it?

Chapter Nine

"You're Gwen Young," Fenella says as she reaches us. "I've seen you in the Avalon Café."

She's tall and well-built, what my mother would have called a horsey type, with brown hair in a ponytail, neutral-coloured makeup, black trousers, and a long-sleeved green sweatshirt. Her accent is refined, without the distinctive west-country burr.

Her face is kind, though, and I give her a smile as I reply, "Yes, that's right. I'm so sorry to intrude; I didn't realize you knew Valerie."

I curl up inside a little with guilt at the lie, but Fenella just says, "Yes. We were... friends." She leaves a fraction of a pause in the middle of the sentence, almost unnoticeable, but I see Arthur glance at me out of the corner of my eye.

"Dylan says that you found her," Fenella continues.

"Yes," I reply. "We were out walking. By the way, this is Arthur..." I realize he doesn't have a surname and have to think on my feet. I can't call him Pendragon... "Penn," I finish, somewhat lamely.

Fenella nods at him. "Nice to meet you."

"And you." Arthur's face is solemn, but I know him well enough now to see the glimmer of humour in his eyes as he glances at me at the announcement of his new surname.

"Please," Fenella says, "come in and have a cup of tea or coffee."

"Can I bring Merlin or would you prefer me to leave him in the car?" I ask.

"He can stay in the kennels," Dylan says, taking his leash from me. "William, our son, will look after him."

I open my mouth to protest, but I can't think what to say, so I let Dylan lead the Labradoodle away. Merlin looks over his shoulder and glares at me. I pull an eek face at him and mouth, "Sorry!"

Arthur and I follow Fenella into the main house. For a moment I think I've entered a scene from Downton Abbey. The place is huge, with tiled floors and a real chandelier hanging from the ceiling beside a large curving staircase. I glance at Arthur, and he raises his eyebrows as we follow Fenella into a big kitchen. It looks spotless; I have a feeling Fenella doesn't cook much herself. Maybe she has a chef come in to do all her food.

"Tea or coffee?" she asks, gesturing for us to take a place at the central pine table.

"Coffee please," we both reply.

"So," she says as she starts preparing the coffee machine, "you found Valerie's body."

"Yes. I was showing Arthur around the abbey, and we just happened to be the first people that entered the Lady Chapel after it happened."

"How awful." She presses the button on the machine, then leans on the counter for a moment, staring out through the window at the kennels. "I can't believe she's gone."

"When did you last see her?" I ask.

"On Saturday." She begins steaming some milk. "A group of us meet up occasionally for lunch. It was Valerie's fortieth next week, and we spent most of the hour discussing her party."

The back door opens, and Dylan comes in, leaving his boots outside. "Merlin's all settled in and having fun," he says.

I refrain from saying *I very much doubt that's the case*, and smile as he joins Fenella in making the coffee. Before long, we're all sipping lattes and nibbling cookies. How strange it is to be sitting there, drinking coffee with Arthur like we're an ordinary couple. Under the table, he rests his hand on mine, and I curl my fingers around his.

"We bumped into Valerie's sister-in-law, Kianna, earlier, in the park," I say. "She was telling us how Valerie hadn't been feeling well lately."

"Yes, that's right." Fenella leans her elbows on the table and sips her drink. "She'd been a bit down. Usually, our weekly meetups are quite fun, but Valerie seemed determined to be a black cloud hanging over us all."

Her words seem quite harsh. Dylan glances at her, but she keeps her gaze on her coffee. I'm sure a woman like Fenella would tell a depressed person to keep their chin up and stop moping around. I can't imagine she's very sympathetic.

"Did she give you the impression she was depressed enough to kill herself?" I ask gently, hoping I'm not probing too deeply.

Fenella shrugs. "It's difficult to say. She didn't like the idea of turning forty. I don't understand that kind of thinking. I hit the big four-oh a few months ago, and it's made no difference to me. You just get on with it, don't you?"

"I know what you mean," I reply politely, still a little puzzled as to her cool manner. I thought they were friends?

Dylan looks at his wife again, then sighs. "If you're wondering why we're not more upset, we had a bit of an argument with Valerie a couple of weeks ago."

Arthur's fingers tighten on mine.

"Oh?" I say.

Fenella visibly stiffens. "It was most unpleasant."

"Valerie brought her Spaniel, Copper, to the kennels while she and her family went to London for a few days," Dylan says.

"I thought her dog was called Beauty?" I reply, confused.

"She had two," Fenella says. "From the same litter—a brother and sister. They both came here. They were fine. Had a whale of a time. But the day after she took them home, Copper fell sick and he died just a couple of days later. Valerie was convinced it was our fault."

"What did Copper die from?" Arthur wants to know.

"The dog had vomiting and diarrhoea, and then I think his heart just stopped. The vet said he could have been poisoned."

"And Valerie blamed you?" I say, trying not to think about Merlin out there in the kennels.

"She said we must have left some rat poison somewhere," Dylan states, "but of course that's ridiculous. We would never keep poison on the site. We're very careful with the dogs that stay here. They were fine until they left. I think it's much more likely that Copper ate something in their garden or in the park."

"It was awful," Fenella says, visibly distressed for the first time since we arrived. "We've run these kennels for over ten years, and I can count the number of complaints we've received on the fingers of one hand. Most dogs adore coming here, and the owners bring them for play dates. It was very upsetting to have one of my best friends accuse us of something like that."

"She must have been very upset," Arthur says.

"I know, that's the main reason why we let it go," Fenella replies. "We eventually managed to persuade her that Copper didn't get the poison from anywhere here, and she apologized, and we agreed to put it behind us. But of course you can't forget something like that."

"No, it must have been quite hurtful."

"It was. We love dogs," Fenella says. "I'd be devastated to think of something happening to one of them while they were staying with us."

"Another cookie?" Dylan asks, lifting the plate and offering it to us. Arthur and I both take one, and he lowers the plate back to the table. Fenella reaches out to help herself, and as she does, the sleeve of her sweatshirt slides up her arm, revealing a small tattoo on the inside of her wrist. It's a black triquetra, and from what I can see, it also has the letters M and S beneath it.

My heart skips a beat. Arthur taps his fingers on mine beneath the table, so I know he's spotted it too.

"Did your other friends know about your argument?" I ask, unable to think of another way to find out who Valerie went to lunch with on Saturday.

Fenella shakes her head and takes a bite of the cookie. "I didn't tell them, anyway. Valerie might have, but nobody mentioned it. We were all too busy talking about the party. Leah and Nancy wanted it to be a medieval costume party, because they worked with Valerie sometimes as actors in the Living History group at the abbey. I wasn't so keen, but of course it was Valerie's birthday and it was three against one, so I was outnumbered."

"Is that Leah Perry?" I ask. She runs the local bookshop in town.

Fenella nods. "And Nancy Armstrong."

Nancy works at Mackenzie's Jewellery Shop, the place I got Arthur's ruby made into a ring. I know both her and Leah to say hello to.

"I am sorry for your loss," I say. "It must have come as quite a shock this morning. I suppose you've been here, working hard." It's a clumsy way to check her alibi, and I wait for her to object.

But she just says, "Yes, Dylan and I get up at six to let the dogs out and give them breakfast. Our son, William, starts work around eight, and we're busy grooming and exercising them for a few hours. To think that I was walking some of the dogs as if I didn't have a care in the world when Valerie was falling from that balcony..." She stops talking and sighs.

I finish off my coffee, and Arthur does the same. "We'd better leave you to it," I say, rising.

"I'll give you a quick tour of the kennels," Dylan says. "Then you can let us know when you want Merlin to stay."

We shake hands with Fenella and head off to the kennels with her husband.

"Please don't judge her," he says as we walk along the garden path. "I know she didn't seem that upset at Valerie's death, but she is really. She's very close with the other women, but that argument with Valerie really upset her."

"Of course. I understand," I reply.

He leads us into the main building, and we discover Merlin sitting at the edge of a room where half a dozen dogs are playing with a young man. Merlin looks like a wallflower, and glares at me as I stifle a chuckle.

"This is Gwen and Arthur," Dylan says. "Merlin's owners."

"He's been very good," says the young man who must be William, Dylan's son. He holds my gaze, his smile widening. He's good-looking, tall, broad-shouldered, and muscular, probably in his early twenties. Fenella said she'd just turned forty, so she must have been very young when she had him.

To my surprise, he winks at me. I drop my gaze, uncomfortable with that flirtatious gesture. I'm hardly old enough to be his mother, but I'm not used to being hit on by men younger than myself.

Dylan shows us around the kennels, pointing out where the dogs sleep and the area where they're groomed, but I already know I'd never bring Merlin here. I wait for as long as seems polite, then say we really must go, and Dylan takes us outside. I don't look at William again as we leave.

Waving goodbye, we head back to the car. I remove Merlin's leash and open the door for him to jump onto the back seat.

"Don't be cross with me," I tell him, bending to kiss his nose.

"He's not cross with you," Arthur says as I go around the car and get in. "He didn't like it there, that's all."

I buckle myself in. "Why not?"

"He didn't like William. Or maybe that was just me." Arthur gives me a wry look. "I saw him wink at you," he says, buckling himself in. "I was tempted to ask if he'd lost his rattle."

I laugh and start the car. "He was very young."

"It was inappropriate of him," he states, somewhat flatly.

"It was. I'm sorry."

"You don't need to apologize. I know men are attracted to you. That doesn't mean I have to like it."

Heat fills my face, and I look away and steer the car out onto the road.

"I'm sorry," he says. "I've embarrassed you."

"No, it's okay." It gives me a warm glow to think he wants me to himself, but I don't want him to think it's okay to be overtly jealous. "So what did you think about them all? It was a strange story about the dog being poisoned, wasn't it?"

Merlin yelps in the back, and Arthur chuckles. "Valerie accused them of poisoning her other Spaniel," he explains to him.

"Do you think they did it?" I ask him.

"I would imagine they're very careful about having poison on the property," he says. "They're right, it was probably more likely that the dog found something in the garden or out in the park."

"Valerie obviously hurt Fenella's feelings, though." I take the first turning at the roundabout. "Do you think Fenella resented her enough to kill her?"

"Who knows?" Arthur says. "She didn't look like a murderer, but then neither did Mary Paxton."

"Good point. What did you think about her alibi?"

"Walking the dogs? I would think she would easily have been able to slip away for half an hour."

I nod. "I could tell you spotted the triquetra tattoo on her arm, by the way."

"Yes. I wonder whether Leah and Nancy have them, too?"

"We might have to investigate," I reply.

He grins at me. "Sounds fun."

"Fancy a trip to the jewellery shop?"

"Sure," he says, so I take the turnoff into town, park the car in the car park by Glastonbury Market Cross, and we walk up the high street.

"By the way," Arthur says, "my surname is now Penn, is it?"

I pull a face at him. "I'm sorry. I'm not great at thinking on my feet."

"It's not a problem. It made me smile." He holds out his hand, and I slide mine into it.

Chapter Ten

Leaving Merlin outside, Arthur and I go into Mackenzie's Jewellery Shop.

It's quiet and cool, with just a couple of customers—a woman looking at an array of watches, and a young guy browsing engagement rings.

Nancy is talking to the woman, so I go over to the counter at the end and wave to James as he looks up from the room where he works out the back. He rises and comes out with a big smile. He's shorter than me, and wider, with a shock of thick grey hair and a bushy grey beard. He could have starred in Mel Gibson's Braveheart. All he needs is a kilt and an axe.

"Gwen! Good morning, how are you?" I love his strong Scottish accent.

"I'm good, thank you. You?"

"Well, thanks." His gaze slides to Arthur, and his smile broadens.

"James," I say, "this is Arthur Penn, for whom you made the ruby ring."

Arthur holds his right hand up to show him where it sits on his little finger, then smiles and holds out his hand, and James shakes it.

"We're lucky it fitted," James says. "You're a big guy, Arthur. Do you need me to resize the ring?"

"No, it's perfect, thank you. You did a beautiful job."

"Well, thank you. It's certainly an interesting stone. Scottish, if I'm not mistaken, and with a very interesting crystalline structure, almost like amber encasing a fly." His eyes are shrewd. I don't know what he suspects, but I'm sure it's not that Arthur's soul is imprisoned inside the gem.

"I don't know much about precious stones," Arthur says cheerfully. "It's a nice colour."

James smiles. "What can I do for you today?"

"Arthur needs a watch," I say. "I thought we'd have a browse."

"Of course." The shop is now empty, and he gestures to his assistant. "Nancy will be pleased to show you whatever takes your fancy."

We move across to the watch cabinets, and I smile at Nancy Armstrong. She's around the same age as Valerie and Fenella—late thirties, early forties, small and slight, with blonde hair cut in a bob, and wearing a white blouse and black skirt. The blouse is long-sleeved, so I can't see if she has a tattoo on her wrist. Pearls adorn her ears, and a couple of expensive-looking rings rest on her fingers. She's not wearing a wedding ring, though.

"Hello, Nancy," I say, and she smiles back. She comes into the café for a coffee sometimes, but we've only ever exchanged pleasantries. "Come on Arthur," I tell him, tugging his arm to pull him to the cabinet. "Come and choose a watch."

He bends over the cabinet, looking at the selection, and I roll my eyes at Nancy. "We might be a while," I tell her, "he's terrible at making up his mind."

"No worries," she replies, "we're quiet at the moment. Take as long as you need."

"Not at work today?" James asks from where he's doing some paperwork by the till. "Don't tell me you've actually got a day off."

"I have. I was showing Arthur around," I tell them. "It was meant to be a fun day, but it didn't start off very well."

"Why?" Nancy asks, taking out a tray of watches as Arthur indicates one that he likes. She removes it and gives it to him. "What happened this morning?"

"Oh, we happened to discover something at the abbey." It suddenly occurs to me that Nancy might not know. I don't want to be the one to tell her.

But her face pales, and she presses her fingers to her lips. "Oh no. You weren't the ones to find Valerie?"

"Yes." I watch James look over in alarm, and he comes around the cabinets to stand next to Nancy, concerned.

"You poor thing," he says, "that must have been awful. We heard about it earlier."

"It was quite a shock." I help Arthur with the clasp of the watch, and he clips it shut, then turns his arm, studying how it looks.

"We were friends," Nancy whispers. "I still can't believe it."

"I told her to go home," James scolds, "but she wouldn't go."

"I'd only sit at home thinking about it." Nancy takes the watch back from Arthur and passes him another to try.

"I'm so sorry," I tell her. "I didn't realize the two of you were friends. I wouldn't have said anything."

"No, it's okay. You weren't to know. Do the police know what happened yet? Did Valerie kill herself?"

"They're investigating now." I shake my head at Arthur as he studies the second watch, and he nods his agreement and takes it off, then taps another one. "We bumped into her sister-in-law, Kianna, this morning. She was telling us that Valerie's been depressed."

"Yes." Nancy undoes the buckle on the leather strap and passes it to Arthur. "She hasn't been herself for a while. We were trying to cheer her up because it would have been her fortieth birthday next week, and we were going to hold a fancy-dress party. She and I were part of the Living History group at the abbey. I work there on Tuesday and Thursday afternoons."

"That must be an interesting job," I say.

"Yes, we all really enjoy it. Leah—that's our other friend who's part of the group—came up with the idea. She suggested that Valerie and Bradley could dress up like a king and queen, and then we could hold a medieval-style banquet. It would have been such fun." Her eyes glisten, and she swallows hard.

"I'm so sorry," I tell her gently. "Do you think she killed herself?"

"I don't know. Maybe. She was very down."

"Do you know why? Was it to do with turning forty?"

"I don't think so. All of us are around the same age. I'll be hitting the big four-oh at the end of the year. She certainly wasn't alone. We talked about it quite a bit, and she seemed okay with it. It was only the last few weeks that she'd been a bit low."

"It must be very hard for you to lose such a good friend. Were you very close?"

"I'd known her a long time."

It's not the straight answer I was expecting, and I exchange a glance with Arthur, who seems taken with the watch with the leather strap. "What's this number?" he murmurs, pointing to the small box with the number twenty-four.

"It's the date," I whisper back. "The twenty-fourth of March."

"Amazing," he says. He turns to James. "I've never seen inside a watch. I don't suppose you have any I could look at?"

James's eyebrows rise. "Of course. I'll fetch you one." He disappears for a moment, then comes back with one he's working on. The back is missing, revealing its mechanism. He and Arthur bend over it, and he gives Arthur an eyepiece so he can study it in detail. I smile, thinking how sometimes Arthur is like a child, fascinated with everything he sees.

I look back at Nancy to find her watching him. I can tell by the look on her face that she finds him attractive. Her gaze comes back to me, and she looks down and starts putting the other watches away.

"Working as part of the Living History team must be fun," I say, brushing aside my irritation.

"It is." She slides the tray back into the cabinet. "They've recently expanded the team, and they've been training us so we can give better guided tours of the site."

Something makes me glance across at the door, and I see Merlin sitting there, looking through the glass at me. He sneezes. My gaze slides back to Nancy.

"Who's in charge of the team?" I ask.

She concentrates on the catch of the last watch. "They interviewed for the role a few weeks ago. Valerie got it." She puts the watch back on the stand and replaces it in the cabinet.

"Did you go for the position?"

"We all did." She closes the cabinet and locks it. "Valerie was always able to talk her way into anything though; it wasn't a surprise that she got the job." She gives me a smile, but she's unable to hide the flicker of resentment she obviously feels.

I have an idea then, and I point to a clock on the wall, almost out of her reach. "I really like that clock. Could I have a closer look at it, please?"

"Of course." She stretches up to retrieve it. As she does so, the sleeves of her blouse fall back. I take a step to the side, just in time to see the black triquetra tattoo on the inside of her wrist before the sleeve covers it again. "Here you go." She places the clock on the table, and I study it for a moment, umm and aah, then tell her I think I'll leave it.

"That is just fascinating," Arthur says, straightening from where he was examining the workings of the watch. "Thank you for sharing that with me. It's so intricate."

"It's rare for someone to appreciate the beauty of the mechanism in this day and age," James remarks.

"Oh, Arthur's a man out of his time," I joke. I join him at the counter and take out my credit card. "You're sure you like this one?" I ask him.

He nods, so Nancy rings up the amount on the till, and I pay for it.

"Well, thank you," I say as Arthur puts the new watch on. "And I'm sorry about Valerie."

"Me too," Nancy says.

"It must have been a shock," I add. "Were you here when you got the news?"

"Yes; I got to work at about a quarter to nine. My coffee break was at eleven, but I didn't take it because a customer had just told us what had happened, and we were all talking about it for a while."

I nod. "Well, I am sorry for your loss. We'll leave you to it now."

"Take care, you two," James says, and we wave and leave the shop.

"Did you see the triquetra?" I ask Arthur as we walk slowly down the high street, Merlin at my side.

"No," Arthur says. "Oh, interesting, so she had one, too."

"Yes. Very mysterious, isn't it? And it's odd; even though Valerie had all these friends, she seems to have had a knack for rubbing them up the wrong way."

"Do you think that Nancy could have had a hand in her death?"

I frown. "I don't know. It's a big jump from being resentful because someone else got the job you wanted to murdering them."

"True. So Nancy had been working there all morning."

"Presumably that gives her an alibi?"

"I guess. I'm sure James would have said if she happened to go out at some point." He lifts his hand and looks at his watch.

"Do you like it?" I ask him softly.

"I love it. But you have to stop spending your money on me."

"Not yet," I tell him. "We need to get you some more clothes first." I take his hand and lead him toward Lilliput's—a small shop that sells menswear. "Come on. Let's get you some basics."

I can think of worse things to do than watch Arthur trying on clothes. When he sees the array of clothing available, it's like watching a kid in a sweet shop. Soon he's trying on jeans, T-shirts, shirts, and sweaters, and each time he comes out of the changing room and poses to show me the result.

We take the final selection to the till, and I add several packets of boxers and socks, and a bottle of nice aftershave. I try not to gulp as the assistant rings up the total and pass her my credit card. I'll have to dip into my savings again, but when it comes down to it, I'm not saving up for anything special, and Arthur can't go without clothes.

We leave the shop with a handful of bags, return them to the car, and I head off home.

"You've spent a lot of money on me today," Arthur says.

"I know. You're worth it." I smile at him.

"That's sweet," he says, "but I can't be a drain on your finances. That's not fair."

"You said you wanted to find a job," I remind him. "You can pay me back later, with interest."

"Interest?"

I explain the concept behind adding interest to a loan. "But I'm joking," I add hastily. "It's the least I can do after waking you up from your slumber."

He studies me thoughtfully for the remainder of the journey, until I start to feel embarrassed by his steady stare.

"What?" I ask, turning onto my road and pulling up outside the house.

"Do you have a shovel?" he asks.

"I... sorry, what?"

"I've got an idea." He smiles. "We're going to dig for buried treasure."

Chapter Eleven

Having no idea what Arthur is planning, I put a shovel in the back of the car, and also my metal detector.

Archaeologists aren't great fans of metal detectors. An important part of archaeology is studying an artefact *in situ*, which means examining the soil around the item, and understanding its place in the site. Knowing the condition and age of the soil and other items above and below an artefact can help to date it, and therefore having amateur treasure hunters pulling precious items out of the ground without recording their surroundings is very frowned on.

But Arthur is determined to find something, so we load up the car, and Arthur finds Google Maps on his phone and pulls up the area.

"Here," he says, showing me the screen.

"Glastonbury Tor?"

"Is it far?" he asks.

I show him how to use the directions option and find out how far it is from one place to another. It states four minutes via the A361 or seven minutes if we take Stone Down Lane through the fields.

"Let's go through the fields," he says, and I set off, turning left into Bove Town and heading out into the countryside.

"There's an article on Glastonbury Tor," he says. "There's a tower on top of the hill?"

"There have been lots of buildings there. Wooden at first, and then the stone Church of St. Michael was built. The tower is what remains of that." I head toward Wick Hollow. "I know archaeologists have found evidence of an Iron Age settlement there, and also signs of Dark Age occupation. I think there was a forge, and several postholes, which indicate a building. Was that when you were there?"

"Yes. People travelled there to make offerings to Taranis, the sky god, and a small village grew up to cater for the visitors."

"It's so strange to hear you talk about those times first-hand," I tell him in wonder. "I've read so much about the Dark Ages, and historians and archaeologists have had to put together events with only one or two pieces of the puzzle."

We emerge from the trees around Wick Hollow, and the countryside opens up. Sheep and their new lambs graze on the hills, while tractors move slowly through the fields, spraying crops and spreading fertilizer. Arthur looks around with interest.

"Does it look familiar at all?" I ask him.

"No," he says. "Much of this land was marsh or river."

"The Tor is in the middle of what we call the Summerland Meadows, which is part of the Somerset Levels. Here's an interesting fact for you." I'm beginning to understand that he likes quirky bits of information. "Sometimes when the ground is marshy or damp, it produces a floating mirage, which makes the Tor look as if it's coming out of the mist. The effect is called a Fata Morgana, which is named after your sister, because the Italians believed she conjured islands in the Strait of Messina to lure sailors to their deaths."

"She'd have liked that," he says. "What a great story." He gestures ahead of us. "There's the Tor."

Sure enough, the mound rises up in front of us, the tower clear against the sky. The road curves around it, but Arthur suggests we park at the bottom of the path leading up to it, so I pull over. We get out with Merlin and retrieve the shovel and the metal detector from the back.

"So we're going up to the Tor?" I ask him uncertainly. There has been a lot of research done around here, and I'm sure archaeologists would have recovered anything he might have left here long ago.

But he says, "No," and he turns and walks off in the opposite direction, carrying the shovel.

I look at Merlin, who licks his nose, and then we both set off after him.

Arthur heads across the field. Relieved that I'm wearing flats and not heels, I almost have to run to keep up with his long-legged stride. He scans the landscape as he walks, a frown on his brow.

"What are you looking for?" I ask. "Some kind of landmark?"

"There used to be an avenue here," he says. "It marked the ceremonial way to the Tor."

"I know where that is," I reply.

He stops and looks at me. "Really?"

"Yes. Two great oaks mark part of it—they're known as Gog and Magog."

His jaw drops. "They're still standing?"

"Sort of. They were cut down to make a farm at the beginning of the twentieth century, but the trunks are still there." I begin walking again, and Arthur follows me.

It's a magical day. It's quiet out here; I can't hear any traffic, and the only sound is birdsong. I spot house sparrows, chaffinches, goldfinches, and a couple of magpies—two for joy! And from the trees in front of us comes the distinctive sound of a cuckoo.

It's warm in the afternoon sun and sweat prickles between my shoulder blades. Summer's coming, and for the first time in ages, I feel excited at the thought of the future. I have so much I want to show Arthur.

"So Gog and Magog were there in the sixth century?" I ask, mainly because I like his voice and want to hear him talk.

He nods. "They were young then, planted only a short time before I first saw them. We came here before the Battle of Camlann. The Saxons had pushed us back repeatedly, and we had to retreat many times. I knew a confrontation was looming. I came here with some of my men, and we buried our coin to keep it safe."

It was a standard practice at the time, and coin hoards have been found all over Britain.

"It's probably been found already," I tell him gently.

"We'll see." For once, he's not smiling, and his eyes hold a kind of grim determination.

We don't speak again for a while. My heart is thumping hard, partly because I'm walking fast, but also at the thought of discovering an ancient hoard, something that belonged to Arthur all those years ago.

In front of us, a tall hedge marks the border of the field. There's a break in it halfway along, with a wooden stile. Arthur vaults over it easily, and Merlin sneaks under it. Arthur turns and holds out his hand, and his fingers close around mine as I navigate the stile and jump down.

"They're just up here," I tell him, and we turn left and walk up the narrow lane. The Tor is behind us now, and it's only a short walk before we see the two old oaks on the right-hand side.

They're only about a third of the height they would have reached, and the trunks are now dead, but they're still impressive. Arthur reaches out a hand and brushes it over the wood. I can't imagine how strange it is for him to connect with a piece of the ancient past that was so young the last time he saw it.

He drops his hand and investigates the hedge between the two oaks. "Through here," he says, and he pushes the branches apart and disappears.

Merlin squirms beneath, and I bend and follow, the tough branches of the hawthorn scratching my cheek. Primroses the colour of butter dot the grass beneath the hedge, and I try not to crush them as I slip through.

I emerge into the field on the other side and stand between the oak trees. "Here," Arthur says, and he unzips his jacket, lets it slide off, and tosses it aside.

"Wait," I say as he goes to pick up the spade. "The detector will tell us if anything metal lies beneath the surface."

I switch it on while Arthur sweeps the ground free of branches and debris in a circle about six feet wide. Then I start to pass the pad of the detector across the ground.

I prepare myself for the disappointment of finding nothing and try to think what to say to Arthur in consolation, but I've barely begun to form the thought when the detector emits a high-pitched beep. My heart bangs against my ribs. If it was iron, the detector would have given a low-pitched beep. There are precious metals beneath the surface of the soil.

Arthur retrieves the spade, walks to where the detector beeps the loudest, and thrusts the spade into the ground. Beside him, Merlin starts digging with his paws.

I watch them, my heart racing, filled with conflicting emotions. I desperately want this to be Arthur's hoard—both for him, and for the excitement of discovering something so important. But part of me feels guilty at the thought of digging up the past like this. I studied archaeology for long enough to know that this is wrong. But how can I tell him to stop now?

The two of them dig for ten minutes, clearing a three-foot-wide square about six inches down, then Arthur stops to tug off his sweater and toss it aside. I stare at the expanse of tanned, muscular chest now visible and swallow hard as he picks up the spade and continues digging. Wow, he's so gorgeous. I'm fascinated by the way his muscles move beneath the surface of his skin. He must have been magnificent on the battlefield, dressed in leather armour, swinging a sword or an axe at the invaders. I'd have followed him anywhere.

It's getting more difficult for him to dig; although he's got rid of the topsoil, the earth contains tree roots and stones, and he has trouble getting the blade into the dirt. But he perseveres, and it's only another ten minutes or so before he's a foot deep.

Merlin stops for a moment, panting. He stands on the edge of the hole, staring down. Arthur grins.

"What's so funny?" I ask.

"He just said, 'A large hole appeared outside the local police station. Officers are looking into it.'"

I giggle. "I bet they still haven't got to the bottom of it."

Arthur's throaty chuckle is infectious, and soon we're both laughing, but it comes to an abrupt halt as he suddenly lets the spade fall and drops to his knees. He reaches out a hand and picks up something, then gets to his feet again and brings it over to me on his palm.

It's a small silver coin.

"Oh dear Goddess." I take it from him and brush the earth away with my thumb. "It's a silver denarius."

"One of many," Arthur says, returning to the hole. He brushes away the earth with his hand, revealing the lip of an urn, and within it more coins protruding through the layer of soil.

"Arthur," I say as he goes to scoop them out. "Wait."

He stops and looks up at me.

"You can't do that," I tell him softly. "I know that to you this is nothing more important than the contents of my money purse, but to archaeologists, this is an incredible find. It needs to be excavated properly, so the coins can be photographed and recorded."

He gets slowly to his feet. "But it's mine. And I want you to have it." He spreads his arms, palms up. He's angry, although I don't think it's with me. "I have nothing," he says, "not even the clothes on my body are mine. I was a rich man, and I put these coins in the ground myself. I want to give you something back, Gwen. I can't expect you to keep me. I have some pride."

"I know." I close the distance between us. "I understand. But this is important to me. I value the past, and anyway, what would we do with the coins if we just dug them up? I can hardly spend them in the shops."

"No, of course not, but you could sell them to a museum."

"They'd want to know where I got them. Look, if we do this right, it's likely you'll get the money anyway. We have specific rules in England. Hidden treasure belongs to the Crown, and failure to report finds to the Coroner can earn you a huge fine and even jail time."

"Seriously?"

"Yes, it shows how important we believe artefacts to be. The coroner holds an inquest to determine if it's treasure. If it is, it'll be valued at the British Museum in London. Museums then bid on it, and they pay a reward that is shared between the finder and the owner of the land on which it was found."

Arthur nods, and I can see understanding dawn in his eyes that these coins are so important, they need to be treated like treasure, not just as money.

I continue, "A similar hoard was found in Frome, not far from here, in 2010. It was valued at over three hundred thousand pounds. The finder received half of that. It's a huge amount of money, Arthur."

"I understand." He brushes his hands free of the soil that is clinging to them. "You must of course do what you think is right. I'm just disappointed because I wanted to give them to you."

"That's incredibly sweet of you, and I'm thrilled to have been with you when you found them."

He looks down as I rest a palm on his bare chest. His skin is warm, and I can feel his heart thudding away. I brush my thumb over the scattering of hair on his ribs. He lifts his gaze and looks into my eyes.

"You're still the most beautiful woman I've ever seen," he says. "The sun on your hair makes it look like fire."

"Oh, Arthur. How do you always know exactly what to say?"

"Years of practice." He smiles. He means years of being with Guinevere—with me.

I slide my arms around his waist, and he lifts his around me. I rest my cheek on his bare chest.

I can smell the fresh earth and the flowers in the hedgerows. The sun casts its warm rays over us, although I don't think that's the reason my skin is heating.

We stand like that for a long time, while Merlin sighs and snuffles about in the leaves, and the cuckoo calls from the ash tree over the lane.

Chapter Twelve

When we get back to town, I park opposite the café and take Arthur to the field unit. Duncan and Una are there, sorting through a box on the big table in the centre. They smile as we walk in, and Una waves.

"Hey Gwen," she says. "How're you doing?"

"We heard you discovered another body this morning," Duncan adds. "I'm so sorry. Are you all right?"

"It was a bit of a shock," I confess, "but I'm okay. Guys, this is Arthur Penn. He's an old friend who's come to stay with me for a bit."

"Hello, Arthur." Duncan shakes his hand, and Una does the same. "It's lovely to meet you."

"Likewise." Arthur peers into the box on the table. "This looks interesting."

"Finds from the Iron Age village near Godney," Una says. "Mainly animal bones. Interesting, though—we think this jawbone is from a brown bear."

"There were bears here in the Iron Age?" Surprised, I address the question to Duncan and Una, but I glance at Arthur and raise my eyebrows. He nods and gives a slight smile. Oh, has he seen one?

"Oh yes," Duncan says. "We think they probably died out around the sixth or seventh century AD."

"I didn't know that." I perch on the table next to the box. "Look, we've found something I think you're going to want to investigate."

"Oh?" They both look up with interest—they know how much I love archaeology, and that even though I don't have a complete degree, I usually know my stuff.

"I took my metal detector out around the Tor, just for fun," I tell them, "and we had a walk up to Gog and Magog. We got a signal between the trees, and when Arthur dug down, we found this." I extract the silver coin from my jeans pocket and hold it out.

Duncan takes it, and he and Una peer at it.

"I don't believe it," Una exclaims, "it looks like a silver denarius."

"That's what I thought. But that's not it. It looks as if there's a whole collection of them in an urn."

Their eyebrows rise and their jaws drop. "How did you leave it?" Una asks.

"We filled in the hole and put some leaves and branches on top of it, which should discourage anyone nosing around. But I think it would be a good idea to rescue it as soon as possible."

"Of course." Duncan looks delighted. "We could go out tomorrow, couldn't we, Una?"

"Absolutely," she replies. "We don't want to leave it where anyone can just dig it up. I think it's John Farlow who owns the field with Gog and Magog in, isn't it? I'll call him and get permission. We could go around ten tomorrow." She smiles at me. "What about you, Gwen? Do you want to come and help us lift it?"

"Oh. Um, well, don't you need... you know... real archaeologists to do that?"

Duncan snorts. "We all know you're as enthusiastic as the rest of us about archaeology. We'd love to have you along."

Una turns the silver denarius over in her fingers. "If there are more silver coins, you know that means it'll be classified as treasure."

"It's treasure to me no matter what the coins are made of," I say happily, thrilled for Arthur's sake that they want to get straight onto it.

"Aw. You're such a sweetie." Una comes around the table and kisses my cheek. "Be here at nine thirty, and you can come with us to meet John and lift the pot."

"Okay." We say goodbye and head outside. "I'm glad we don't have to wait long," I say to Arthur as we return to the car.

"It'll be interesting to see what they have to say." Arthur is hiding his disappointment well. I'm incredibly touched that he wants to contribute to the income, but pleased he's willing to wait to do it the right way.

"I suppose we should go home," I say, a little reluctantly. It's been a full day, and we've managed to cram a huge amount into it, but I'm sure he must be tired.

"I thought you'd want to go and see Valerie's other friend first," he says.

"Leah? You're sure you're not too tired?"

"I don't seem to get tired," he says. "I'm sure I will eventually, but at the moment I don't think I can sleep."

"All right, then. Let's go and speak to Leah. Then we'll go home and have dinner."

We walk around the building and down the high street. It's about four thirty, so a few shops are getting ready to close, and a couple of the daytime cafés are shut. Perry's Bookshop is still open, though. A young woman is behind the till, serving a customer. Leah Perry is at the back of the shop, sorting through a new delivery.

She's medium height, with shoulder-length brown hair and a pair of rectangular black-rimmed glasses. I know her to say hello to, when she comes into the café occasionally for a coffee, and she smiles at us as we walk up.

"Hello," she says. "Gwen, isn't it? From the Avalon Café?"

"Yes, that's right. This is Arthur," I reply, and he nods to Leah.

"How can I help?" she asks, straightening from where she's sorting through a box of books.

"Can you direct us to the local section? I was hoping to get Arthur a book on his namesake's connection to the area."

She smiles. "Of course. It's over here." She leads us across the bookshop to a stand marked 'Local History'. "This is a good one," she says, reaching up to collect a book called *Arthur's Isle*. She's wearing a three-quarter-sleeved sweater, and as she turns her hand to pick up the book, she reveals the small black triquetra tattoo on the inside of her wrist, complete with the letters M and S.

Arthur glances at me, then takes the book from her as she holds it out and starts leafing through it.

Leah clears her throat and rubs her nose. "I hope you don't mind me saying, but I heard that you discovered the body of Valerie Hopkins-Brown this morning."

"That's right, yes. We were taking a walk through the Abbey and just happened to be the first to find her."

"How awful for you," she says. "I can't believe it. I only saw her a couple of days ago."

"Actually," I admit, "I was talking to Fenella Davies earlier today. We took my Labradoodle, Merlin, over for a visit and got chatting, and she mentioned that she met with Valerie and you and Nancy Armstrong. She said you were planning her birthday party."

"That's right." Leah looks downcast. "It would have been such fun. The Lady of the Lake pub has a room out the back, and sometimes they do medieval meals—things like roast pig, and you eat off bread trenchers and drink ale out of tankards. We were all going to wear our Living History dresses. It would have been marvellous."

"I'm so sorry," I say gently, as she looks genuinely upset. "Forty is no age at all."

"It's really not. People go on about it as if it's the end of the world, but she wasn't that upset about it."

"Oh? I heard she'd been a bit low over the past few weeks, that's all."

"She had, but I don't think it was about turning forty."

"Did she have other problems, then?" I know I'm probing, and I wait for her to tell me to mind my own business, but she leans forward conspiratorially.

"I don't want you to think I'm not upset about what's happened," she says. "I am—I'm devastated. We'd known each a long time. And I'm not normally a bitchy kind of person."

"Well," I reply, "I know they say about not speaking ill of the dead, but when someone dies, it doesn't make them a saint."

"That's right." She seems pleased I understand. "The thing is, she could be quite a difficult person. She was nice on the surface, and always keen to help wherever she could, but she could be confrontational at times, and when she wanted something, she could be very... determined."

"Fenella mentioned something similar," I reveal.

"Yes, of course, they had a run-in several weeks ago about Valerie's Spaniel that died. That was quite unpleasant. They made up, but that kind of thing doesn't go away, does it?"

"No. And Nancy mentioned that Valerie got the position as head of the Living History team. There seems to have been a bit of bad feeling there, too."

"Nancy really wanted it," Leah admits. "She reads a lot of history books and watches all the archaeological programmes on TV, and I think she thought she was going to get it, but Valerie could be very charming, and I'm sure she talked her way into it."

A bit like her brother, I think to myself. Matthew can be quite the smoothie when he wants to be.

Arthur puts the book back on the shelf. "I would have thought you would have been a good contender for head of the team, working here. You obviously read a lot of history books, too."

Leah shrugs. "I went for the job, but I'm not devastated that I didn't get it. I'm busy here, and doing the Living History tours is fun, but I don't want it to take over the shop. I'm also running for the Board of Governors at the high school—I'm hoping to be chairperson."

"Wow," I say, "that's a challenging role."

"Valerie and I were both going for it," she says. "I suppose I stand a better chance now." She meets my eyes. "Sorry, that was inappropriate. I meant it to be funny, but it came out as callous—I really didn't mean it like that."

"It's okay, I understand." I give her a sympathetic smile. "Her death must have been a real shock for you. Were you here when you got the news?"

"Yes, I get to the shop around eight thirty. I'd had a new delivery, and Casey and I worked here cataloguing the books non-stop until around midday." She nods toward the girl at the desk.

I look at Arthur. "Well, did you want any of these books?"

"I think I'll get this one," he says, holding up *Arthur's Isle*. "It's very informative and has some nice photos, too."

"Okay." I take it from him and smile at Leah. "Thanks for your help, and I'm very sorry about your friend."

"Thank you." She smiles back, and we leave her to go back to her unpacking while we pay for the book and then head out.

We walk slowly back to the car, Merlin at our heels. "What do you think?" I ask him. "Valerie does seem to have rubbed quite a few people up the wrong way."

"So they were both hoping to be on the Board of Governors for the school," he says. "I'm not quite sure what that is, but it doesn't sound like a position worth killing someone for."

"I wouldn't have thought so. I wouldn't have thought any of the problems that Valerie's friends had would provoke them to murder, but someone must have done it." I hold my hand out to Arthur, who takes it in his own. "Are you hungry?"

"I seem to be permanently ravenous," he admits.

I chuckle. "Let's go home, then, and I'll cook you a nice dinner. What would you like to eat?"

"I have no idea. What choices do I have?"

I get him to pull out his phone and give him some options to look up. He's excited at the range of exotic dishes I'm able to prepare—recipes from all around the world, including Japan, China, and India.

"What does curry taste like?" he asks. "It sounds very popular in England."

"It's England's most loved food," I tell him as I park the car outside the house, "adopted from when India was part of the British Empire. Curry is amazing. It's usually spicy, though. Do you like spicy food?"

"I don't know," he says. "Probably."

Laughing, I let us indoors. We take off our jackets and shoes and go into the kitchen, and Arthur sits at the table and reads his new book while I cook. Occasionally he reads out paragraphs to me or shows me photographs, commenting on what the place looked like in his time.

It's only been a day since he came to life, but as I fry onions and chicken, and add spices and tomato paste and cream to the sauce, it occurs to me that I feel as if I've known him forever. I don't feel weird being at home with him alone anymore. It's almost as if we've been married for years.

Chapter Thirteen

It turns out that Arthur likes curry.

"Do you think there's anything you're not going to like?" I ask him with amusement, as I watch him wipe up the last drops of sauce with a piece of homemade naan bread.

"No," he says, chewing and then giving me a grin. "You're an amazing cook, Gwen. I've watched you for all these years producing fantastic cakes and pies and thought they were wonderful, but you truly are talented."

"I'm really not," I scoff, rising to collect his plate and taking it with mine over to the dishwasher. "Anyone can make a decent curry. It's really easy."

He watches me, his eyes holding that lazy, sexy look that suggests he's wondering what I look like without my clothes.

"Stop it," I scold, squirting washing-up liquid into the bowl to clean the pan. "I've known you one whole day. You can't look at me as if you have x-ray vision."

"What's that?"

"As if you're wearing glasses that can see through my clothes."

"Is there such a thing?" His voice holds wonder and hope.

"No." I laugh. "I'm sure you'd buy a pair if there was."

"Absolutely I would. What man wouldn't?" He chuckles and rises to pick up the tea towel and dry the items I put on the draining board.

I cast a sidelong glance at him. "This is weird."

"What is?"

"Washing up with King Arthur."

"I told you, I wasn't a king. But I don't mind if you want to call me that."

I nudge him. He nudges me back. Merlin snorts from under the table, and we both laugh. I glance over my shoulder at him. "It's funny to think he was a bard."

"And a good one at that."

"He composed poems?"

"And sang them while he played the lute. He had a lovely singing voice." Arthur's gaze drifts off for a moment, and I wonder whether he's picturing an evening sitting around the fire with his soldiers, listening to songs of home.

"Do you want to hear one?" Arthur says.

I blink. "What do you mean?"

He picks up a plate and dries it while he sings. He has a deep, rich voice that sends shivers all the way through me.

"Sparks in the hearth, stars in the sky, singing an endless lullaby, your love is a golden thread through the weft and weave, a fairy tale I'll always believe, leaving you is a sword that pierces the heart, the wind and the rain and the heavy snows… that fall on the fields and the valleys and the hills… will never keep us apart…" He holds the last note, then stops and smiles.

"Oh," I say breathlessly, looking down at Merlin, "that's beautiful."

The Labradoodle lies with his snout on his paws, his big brown eyes looking up at me.

"Who was it about?" I ask softly. "He obviously loved her very much."

Arthur looks down at the dog, then back up at me. He doesn't say anything, just reaches for another plate to dry.

My mouth opens. "M-me?"

"He was soft on you," Arthur says. "We never discussed it, but it was obvious."

"Aw." I drop to my knees and bend to kiss the dog's head.

"Don't feel sorry for him," Arthur tells me. "More than his share of beautiful women passed through his tent flap."

That makes me giggle, and I'm convinced Merlin rolls his eyes. I kiss him again, then rise and return to washing the dishes, humming the song.

When I'm done, I dry my hands and tell Arthur, "I need to make a couple of phone calls. I should ring Immi and Beatrix. Then we can settle down for the evening. Maybe watch a movie?"

"I'd like that."

I pour us both another glass of wine, and we take them into the living room. Arthur chooses a book from the shelves—my well-thumbed copy of Shakespeare's plays—and sits in one of the armchairs to read it, Merlin at his feet, while I stretch out on the sofa, my feet up, and call Imogen.

"It's me," I tell her when she answers.

"Hey, you. How are you doing?" I can hear the rustling of papers; she's still in the office.

"Why aren't you out on a date with Christian?" I scold.

"Too much work," she says. "It's good to keep 'em waiting."

"No it's not. Arthur and I want to know if you and Christian would like to go to dinner with us."

"Really?" She sounds delighted. "I'd love that. When?"

"What are you doing tomorrow night?"

"Working."

"Then tomorrow it is. I'll book us a table at 'I Long for Won Ton' for seven. I think Arthur's going to like Chinese. He had curry tonight and wolfed the lot."

Over in his chair, Arthur gives a short laugh.

"I knew he'd like curry," Imogen says. "He's a real man's man."

"He is. Very." I study his handsome face, thinking about what it would be like to kiss him.

Without moving his head, his gaze rises to meet mine for a moment before he smiles and returns it to his book.

"How are the two of you doing?" Imogen wants to know. "It's a shame the day started off so badly. Has it got any better?"

"Oh yes, definitely."

"I knew it," she says. "You kissed him, didn't you?"

"No. Not yet. We had a hug, though."

"You two are so sweet. So what have you been up to?"

"Well… I hope you won't be cross, but we've been doing a little investigating."

"Into Valerie? I don't mind at all. Saves me a job."

I tell her what we've been up to today, about how we discovered she'd had lunch with her friends, and what each of them had to say.

"Goodness," she says when I'm done, "you have been busy."

"We have. It was a very productive day. Is any of it useful?"

"I'm sure it will be. I'm waiting for the coroner's report to come back. I'm still not sure whether her death was an accident or not. The presence of your watch suggests it wasn't, but that's not enough evidence to go on. I've spent most of the day dealing with Bradley and the rest of her family, and going over the evidence from the scene. If it becomes clear that she was murdered, what you've told me today will give me a good foundation for an investigation." She pauses. "What conclusions have you drawn from it?"

Imogen knows almost everything about me. She knows I'm a witch, and she knows I rescued Arthur from Sir Boss. I helped her solve Liza Banks's murder, and she's been very open to everything I've thrown at her. But I don't know how she'll feel about the fact that my Labradoodle is psychic.

"I've got something to tell you," I say cautiously. "You've been great so far in believing me, but this might take a stretch of the imagination."

"I can't wait. Go on."

"Well, you know I told you about The Star Sign Spell that Mary Paxton placed on Liza to chain her soul to this plane. That's why we saw her ghost."

"Yes."

"Last night, Arthur and Merlin were able to release her."

She went silent for a moment. "How?" she says eventually.

"I'm not quite sure how they did it. But Arthur told me that Merlin is the spirit of a bard—like a troubadour, a poet. And Morgana taught him how to help people pass on to the Summerlands—that's what he calls heaven. And that's what he does; he communicates with the souls of those chained to this plane and does what he can to help them pass on."

"Wow. Really?"

"Yes."

"And so… with Valerie…"

"Yes, he's seen her. And I saw her too, this morning, in the crystal ball. It's too much of a coincidence. Immi, I'm convinced she was murdered. I know you can't use any of this as evidence in court, but anything I can do to help, just say."

"Of course. So… do you think there's something supernatural about her death, the way there was with Liza?"

"I'm suspicious, mainly because Fenella, Nancy, and Leah all had the triquetra tattoo on the inside of their wrists."

"Oh! Goodness, well spotted. That definitely needs to be noted." I hear her tapping on her keyboard. "Thank you for that."

"I promise not to interfere with your investigation, but I hope I can help."

"Of course you help, Gwen. People talk to you in a way that they don't to me. You've already discovered that all three of her friends have a motive for murder. Or at least, a motive for disliking her."

"I can't imagine that any of them killed her, but then again I didn't think Mary looked like a murderer, so…"

"I know what you mean," she says. "I took a look at the video footage from last night of the Interactive Museum at the Adventure. Mary does something, doesn't she, to block the view of the cameras? Some kind of spell?"

"Yes, she's quite skilled."

"I was worried she'd turn me into a frog."

I laugh. "Just make sure her hands are clean. Magic takes ingredients—herbs and flowers, that kind of thing."

"Okay, I will. I'd better go—things to do, and it would be nice to get home before midnight. But I'll see you tomorrow?"

"I'll book the restaurant now. Take care, Immi."

We hang up. Then I dial the number for 'I Long for Won Ton' and book a table for the following evening.

"That will be fun," I tell Arthur when I'm done. "I'm looking forward to that."

He puts his book down. "It'll be interesting to talk to Christian. I like him. He helped you a lot when Alice died."

"I got in a muddle with some of the paperwork. He was very kind."

"I was thinking," he says. "You'll be busy in the morning going with Duncan and Una to collect the urn. I wondered whether you could ask Beatrix if I could see Max and have a chat about any positions he might have."

My eyebrows rise. "Don't you want to come with me and watch the urn being lifted?"

"Not really," he says. "It makes me feel… odd."

I think about that for a moment. Fifteen hundred years ago, he dug a hole and placed the urn intact into the earth. Now it's old and crumbling, and people are going to be picking over the coins and selling them to a museum. They were his property, and he wanted me to have them. No wonder he feels odd.

"All right," I say softly. "I'll call Beatrix."

I ring her number, then sit back, watching him pick up his book again. He's coping with all this remarkably well, but I still have to give him space to come to terms with it all. He's only human.

"Gwen!" Beatrix says, sounding pleased. "Lovely to hear from you. We've been wondering what kind of day you've both been having."

"Busy," I say. "You're never going to guess what happened to us this morning."

We chat for a while about finding Valerie's body, and I summarize our day, and the things we've discovered.

"Wow," she says eventually. "You were right—you have been busy. I'm so sorry your day had to start like that, though."

"It was a shame, but these things happen. Look, I have something to ask you. Or rather, for you to ask Uncle Max. I've been talking to Arthur, and he's keen to get a job. He wants to be able to contribute some income."

"He's a real sweetheart," she says. "You hang onto him, darling."

I blush and study my fingernails as Arthur looks up. "Well, anyway, I don't want to put Max on the spot, but I wondered if he'd be able to look around for a position for Arthur? I know he doesn't have our formal qualifications, but he's good with his hands."

"Really?" she teases.

"Beatrix!" I blush even harder, and Arthur chuckles. "I meant with carpentry. I thought Max might know someone who can find him a job."

"As it happens, we were talking about that today. Max can definitely find him work. He suggested he show Arthur around the business and have a chat with him, see what he'd like to do."

"He'd love that," I say, delighted they're able to help.

"Wonderful. I'll get Max to pick him up tomorrow. Eight thirty?"

"Yes, thank you. He'll be ready."

"All right. Well you take care of yourselves. Are you getting on okay?"

"Yes," I say softly. "Very well."

"I'm glad, dear. It's only what you deserve. Let us know if you need anything else."

"I will. Bye."

I hang up and look over at Arthur. He closes his book, leans his head on a hand, and smiles at me.

"You're going to work tomorrow," I tell him. "Eight thirty."

"Great," he says. "I look forward to it."

I shake my head. "You're so new to this world. Don't you want to get on a plane and travel? Go exploring? Discover all the amazing inventions and people and places?"

"We will," he says. "You're the most important thing to me. First, we need to get to know each other. Then we can explore the rest of the world."

I pick up my wine and sip it as I study him. "What was Guinevere like? Are we similar at all?"

"Of course you're similar. You are her."

I purse my lips. "Oh. I suppose so. I'm having trouble getting my head around that. I guess it's as if I have amnesia. Maybe that's the way I should be thinking about it."

He smiles. "I don't think so. We both have to think of this as a new relationship. I don't expect you to fall in love with me just because I tell you we were once lovers. It might be that this time around, you don't feel the same way as you did before. I will do my best to win you all over again, but you can't force love."

"No," I reply, "you can't. Equally, if you get to know me and decide your feelings have changed, we're not married. You're not bound to me."

He gives me a wry smile that says, *You really have no idea.* But he just states, "Time will tell."

Our eyes lock, and I can't look away. I keep having to remind myself I've only known him for one day. Neither of us should be making any decisions this early in a relationship. We barely know each other.

So how come what I feel for him is so strong? So deep?

I need to slow down, because I don't want my heart to be broken. But it's hard to fight against what feels like fate.

"Shall we watch a movie?" I ask, desperate to change the subject.

He nods. "I'd love to."

"Come over here, then, and we'll choose one. What kind of thing would you like? A thriller? Adventure? Historical? Comedy?"

"Something romantic," he says.

Smiling, I choose *Sleepless in Seattle*. Arthur holds up his arm, and I curl on the sofa beside him and rest my head on his shoulder, then sneak my arm around his waist, while Merlin stretches out in front of us.

For the rest of the movie, we barely move an inch.

Chapter Fourteen

By ten a.m. the next day, I'm in the process of helping Duncan and Una excavate the urn holding Arthur's coins. The farmer allowed us access to the field, and Duncan drove the car up to the site between the oak trees so he could unload the equipment.

It's a gorgeous spring morning. I'm thoroughly enjoying myself, although I miss Arthur more than I would have thought possible. Max picked him up this morning, and Arthur kissed me on the cheek before he left, making me blush as Max smiled and turned away to give us some privacy.

"I'll miss you," Arthur murmured.

"Me too," I whispered back, and I had to restrain myself not to run after him as he got in the car and Max pulled away.

I suppose part of my unease is the fear that he's going to vanish as quickly as he arrived, and I'll never see him again. I like him so much. And what girl wouldn't love the way he seems to adore me, and want to do anything for me? It's like a perfect bubble, floating on the spring breeze, but I'm terrified it's going to pop and I'll be left with nothing but a memory of his beautiful blue eyes.

I push the fanciful feelings away and concentrate on the rich earth before me. I'm not going to get depressed over something that hasn't happened yet, and might never happen at all.

"Okay," Duncan says as we finally remove the layer of topsoil that Arthur and I had filled in the day before. "Let's take some photos."

It's a painstaking process. Merlin sits at the edge of excavation, apparently content to watch as we mark the area with tape measures to indicate the size of the site, then begin to remove the soil, taking photos every time we find another coin. Every trowel-full of soil that comes out is sieved, and we place any objects we find into clear plastic bags and write on them a number, so we know in what order they came out.

It's not long before we uncover the lip of the urn and the top of the coins inside the pot. We put our trowels aside, and then we're on to brushes, carefully flicking away tiny fragments of soil to reveal the coins.

They're muddy, of course, the surfaces obscured, but I can see that most of them are bronze, with the occasional silver one shining through. We remove the loose ones on the top, but Una wants to keep as many of them inside the pot as we can, so now we begin digging around the edge of the pot, continuing to sift the earth to make sure we don't lose any of the coins.

It's a slow process, but I'm happier than I've been for a long time, my hands covered in earth, listening to the birdsong and chatting to the two of them about archaeology as we work. I know they don't want to leave the pot half-excavated overnight, and they're going to want to lift it today, so even though it's tough on my back and knees, I stay with them, stopping only for a sandwich at lunchtime before we carry on.

At regular intervals, Arthur texts me. The first one makes me laugh.

Max showed me how to text, so here I am. This is amazing! I can talk to you even though you're miles away! I love the twenty-first century. A x

I chuckle and reply, *How are you getting on? Does Max have a suitable position for you?*

Definitely, he replies. *I can work here while I take a carpentry and joinery course, so I have a proper qualification, but he says I know most of the work already. I'm going to start next week.*

I'm so glad. *And the two of you are getting on all right?* I ask. It's important to me that they like each other. Max married Beatrix when I was a toddler, so I've known him as long as I can remember, and he's very important to me. And of course, I want him to like Arthur.

He's a top fellow, Arthur replies. *We're going for a beer after work. I'll be home in time for our meal out, though.*

That makes me laugh. He's really fitting into modern working life.

By mid-afternoon, we've removed the earth around the urn, sketched and photographed the site, sieved all the earth and removed any loose coins and other objects, and we're ready to lift it.

"It's going to be heavy," Una warns.

So Duncan comes up with the idea of crafting a sling from one of the tarpaulins he keeps in his car to cover a dig if it starts raining. He folds it in half and slides it into the hole beside the urn, and we tip it onto its side as far as we can before each taking a corner and pulling together. It is super heavy, but after ten minutes of hard work, we finally have it out and on the ground.

Duncan immediately rights it and ties the tarpaulin around it to ensure no other coins fall out, and then we lift it into his car. Finally, we fill in the hole with earth and loose stones from around the site.

When we're done, and Duncan starts covering the site with leaves and twigs, I take the shovel back to the car and close the hatchback's boot. I'm just about to turn away when a strange wind whips across the site, making me pause. In the reflection of the window, I can see Duncan behind me, tidying the site, and clouds scudding across the blue sky.

And then, as if it's one scene in a movie fading to the next, the sky darkens, and suddenly it's night-time. Duncan vanishes, but in his place two men appear.

One has long grey hair braided and fastened at the nape of his neck with a silver clasp, and lines around the corners of his eyes. He's wearing dark red trousers and a green tunic. He holds the urn of coins in his hands, and he's watching the other man, who's digging the ground in the same place that we just were.

The second man is taller, with longish dark hair and a thick beard. He's stripped to the waist, his body shining with sweat in the moonlight. He lifts his head and his eyes meet mine, and I feel a sharp connection between us, like a bee sting—a tug in my solar plexus.

It's Arthur.

"Ready, Gwen?" Duncan asks.

I blink, and the two men vanish. The sky clears, and it's daylight again.

My mouth has gone dry, but I manage to mutter, "Yes, of course." I open the door for Merlin to hop in, and I get in beside him.

All the way back, Una and Duncan chat with excitement about the find, but I look out of the window, feeling oddly detached and unable to concentrate. We return to the field unit, and they ask me if I want to help remove the coins from the urn, but I'm on edge and too restless to work. I thank them for the great day, call in at the café to make sure everything's running smoothly, then head home.

I stand in the kitchen, feeling Arthur's absence in every bone in my body, even though I've only spent one day with him. Merlin comes up and nuzzles my hand, and I bend and put my arms around him.

"Was that you?" I whisper. "The other man in my vision? Taliesin the bard?"

He licks my face, and I give a shivery sigh. Did I really have a glimpse into the past, over fifteen hundred years ago? The moment when Arthur put the urn into the ground? It's hard to believe, and yet why is it any more impossible than having him come back to life?

I stand and look out at the garden. It's always brought me comfort when I'm feeling out of sorts. So I pick up my gardening gloves and head outside into the spring afternoon.

I work there for a couple of hours, mowing the lawn, then doing some weeding in the veggie patch. There's something about gardening that enables your body to work automatically, leaving your brain to work through things like a computer left to run its own program.

As I slide the trowel into the rich earth and pick out the tiny weeds, I think about my day, uncovering the silver coins between Gog and Magog, so long after Arthur first buried them. It was almost as if he sent them to himself in the future, like a message in a bottle. A fanciful notion, but I like it.

I think about the brooch of his in the museum, and the look of joy on his face when he saw it. The threads that link us to each other in life continue on, weaving through time. The Books of Shadows I have indoors, written by my ancestors, are similar—Josephine, Harriet, Lizzie, and Alice; the notes they wrote all those years ago are messages they delivered to me as sure as if they tied them to the leg of a pigeon and sent them through time.

I work, parting the earth, pulling weeds, removing stones. Rich earth, thick and moist, like chocolate muffin mix being turned with a wooden spoon. My baking is more than combining flour and eggs and herbs. It carries within it those threads of time; the experiences of my mother and grandmother, the knowledge they've passed to me, either directly through their books, or indirectly, through their DNA. A message in a bottle...

I feel a little drowsy; it must be the sun. I sit back on my heels, shade my eyes, and look at the greenhouse, just a few feet away. The nearest glass pane to me is bright in the sunlight. I can see Merlin lying on the grass beside me, his snout on his paws. His brown eyes are watching me.

And beside him, lying on the grass, is a woman in white, covered with colourful flowers.

My heart bangs against my ribs, and I inhale sharply. Merlin stands, and then he looks down at the woman, so I know he can see her, too. We both watch as, very slowly, she sits up and looks at me, then stands. The flowers fall to the ground and disappear.

Her blue eyes stare into mine for a long moment. I'm breathing fast, my heart racing at a million miles an hour. Then, unable to stop myself, I turn my head to look at Merlin on the grass behind me. He's there, but the woman isn't. I look back at the greenhouse. She's vanished.

Merlin sits, telling me that he can't see her, either.

"Oh Goddess," I say. "I didn't expect that. Why did she appear to me?" But I don't really have to ask the question.

Something's happening to me; I can feel it. My supernatural abilities are slowly blooming, like a rosebud unfurling its petals in the sun. Perhaps it was connecting with Arthur in the sixth century. Or maybe it was realizing today how much I'm connected to the women in my family who've gone before me. They've handed down more than their recipes in their Books of Shadows. I have their genes, and they carry magic within them, all through the generations, maybe all the way back to Alice Young in the seventeenth century who was hanged for witchcraft here in Glastonbury. And maybe back even further, all the way to Guinevere and Morgana.

The Labradoodle gets up, comes over, and nuzzles my hand. "It's all right," I tell him. "I'm not scared." If anything, I feel excited, enlivened. It's as if I've been asleep, like Arthur, for so long, and now I'm just starting to wake.

Chapter Fifteen

"Honey, I'm home!"

I hear Arthur calling inside the house, and I smile, go indoors, and wash my hands in the sink. Arthur comes into the kitchen, Uncle Max behind him.

"Did Max tell you to say that?" I ask.

"He did." He walks over to kiss my cheek

"You should have a shower," I tell him, blushing. "We'll be going out soon."

"All right." He holds his hand out to Max, who shakes it. "Thank you for today," Arthur says.

"You're more than welcome," Max replies.

"I'll see you Monday morning, then?"

"Absolutely."

Arthur smiles, then disappears upstairs.

"Do you want to sit down?" I ask Max.

"No, I'll get going in a minute. I know you're going out." Max leans a hip on the kitchen counter and smiles at me.

"So… How was he today?" I ask softly. I'm not comfortable talking behind Arthur's back, but I wouldn't be human if I didn't want to know what Max thinks of Arthur.

"You've fallen on your feet there, girl. He's solid and dependable, exactly the kind of guy I'd want for you."

"Oh, I'm so glad you like him."

"I like him because you like him. But I know what you mean." He comes over to me and gives me a hug. His white beard tickles my cheek. "I do worry about you," he whispers. "You've been through so much. I'm glad you have someone to watch over you now."

I swallow hard. "I hope that's the case."

He moves back a little. "What do you mean?"

"Only that I can't shake the feeling that he's going to vanish suddenly. I'm… afraid to hope, you know?"

Max rubs my upper arm. "I'm sure that's not the case," he soothes. "He's travelled through time to be with you. That sounds like a long journey, and not one he can—or would want to—repeat."

"I suppose."

"I'm really glad to have him on the team. He's a hard worker, and he has a wide range of skills."

"He said something about taking a course in carpentry?"

"Actually," Max says, "I'm considering more of a general training course for him. For some time now, I've been thinking about putting together a team of handymen, a kind of odd-job squad. You'd be surprised how many calls we get from people wanting small things done around the house—shelves put up, doors fixed, dripping taps mended. I think it would be perfect for Arthur—flexible enough so he can be there if you need him, but a reliable source of income so he feels he's contributing."

"It sounds great," I say, although I feel a twinge of doubt. Will the man who led a whole army—the infamous King Arthur—be content being an odd-job man?

Max kisses my forehead. "I'd better go. I have to drag Beatrix out of the studio every evening or else she'll be there all night."

I laugh and go with him to the door. "See you later."

He waves and goes to his car.

I go back inside and climb the stairs to my bedroom. It's time to get ready for our evening with Imogen and Christian. I'm really looking forward to it.

At the top of the stairs, I meet Arthur coming out of the shower, a towel wrapped around his waist.

"Oh!" I stop and stare at the expanse of his chest—the shiny, tanned muscles, the light-brown hairs that glisten with drops of water.

After an awkward few seconds, I finally manage to elevate my gaze to meet his.

"Something wrong?" he says. His eyes are warm.

I look down at Merlin. I can almost hear him laughing.

"Wait," Arthur says. "Merlin says you had another vision?"

I nod and explain about how I saw Valerie's ghost in the garden.

"Your talents are waking up," Arthur says. "I told you that you were powerful." I hesitate, and he tips his head to the side. "What?"

"I saw something else earlier, at the dig site. I had a vision of a dark night, and of two men putting the urn into the ground. One of the men was you. You looked right at me, and something happened… I felt a kind of… connection all the way back to you."

He stares at me for a long moment. Then he says softly, "I remember."

"Remember what?"

"That night. I saw you, too. I'd forgotten."

My eyes widen. "Really?"

"I was about halfway through digging the hole, and I glanced up and you were standing there. I thought it was Guinevere—you looked just like her, although I remember thinking that your clothes were strange. It was only brief, but yes, our eyes met, and I felt the same connection. I mentioned it to her later, after the battle, but she didn't seem to know what I was talking about, and I forgot about it."

"That was the night before the Battle of Camlann?" I ask, knowing that was where he was mortally wounded.

"Yes."

We look into each other's eyes for a long moment.

He moves a little closer to me. "I think it was that connection that drew me to you, all these years later. We were already husband and wife, but at that moment, being in exactly the same place, somehow our souls connected in a way that was going to bind us together forever."

Tears come into my eyes. "What a lovely thing to say."

He smiles. "I know this is all new to you. And I know you need time. But there's something special between us, Gwen. And it's not going anywhere anytime soon, so you'd better get used to it."

The look in his eyes is firm, lazy, sexy. He completely intends to have me. I don't think I'm going to have much say in the matter.

And now I feel a little faint.

"Who was the other man with you?" I ask, trying to distract him before I pass out. "Was that Taliesin?"

He looks down at the dog. "Yes. He was with me that night. I told him I saw a vision of you. He just smiled and said 'You two are one, Arthur. Are you really surprised?'"

I bend and kiss the top of Merlin's head, feeling warm all the way through. "We'll be late," I murmur. "I'd better get ready." I slip by them into my room. As I turn, I see them both watching me before I close the door.

I sit on the bed and wait for a minute or two until my heart stops racing. What a strange day. Half of me is thrilled at the thought of being part of a romance that has survived so many years. The other half feels a little overwhelmed and a touch panicky. I'm already crazy about Arthur, and possibly more than a little in love with him. But everything's moving so fast, and I'm frightened of letting my hopes get too high, only to have them dashed on the rocks. I don't want to be hurt.

Gently does it, I tell myself. I don't have to do anything I'm not ready for. We can still take our time to get to know each other. I just need to relax.

Within fifteen minutes, I'm ready, and I go downstairs and discover the two of them in the living room. Like any twenty-first-century man, Arthur's on his phone, probably researching something. Merlin's sitting beside him on the sofa like a person, looking over his arm at whatever's on the screen.

Arthur's wearing some of the new clothes we bought him—a pair of dark-blue jeans, and a white casual shirt with a thin blue stripe. Wow. He looks amazing.

They both look up as I come into the room, and I have the pleasure of watching surprise and admiration pass over Arthur's face as he sees me. I look down at my outfit—I'm wearing a floor-length midnight-blue velvet skirt, and a light blue top with a slight shimmer in it. It's a bit of a hippy outfit, but it suits the Glastonbury vibe.

My hair is down, falling almost to my bottom in soft red waves. Arthur rises from the sofa, comes over to me, and lifts a strand, letting it slip through his fingers. "Like fire," he murmurs.

"Come on," I say softly, stifling a shiver. "Time to go."

We leave Merlin at home by the hearth. He's tired, and I know he'll be asleep in minutes. Arthur and I then walk the short distance to town.

Imogen and Christian are just walking up as we approach 'I Long for Won Ton'. "Hello, you two," Imogen says. She's wearing a skirt, for once, with a pretty green blouse, and her hair is down, bouncing around her shoulders in chocolate waves.

She kisses me and smiles at Arthur, then gestures at Christian. "Christian, this is Arthur. Arthur, Christian."

The two men shake hands, and Imogen and I exchange an amused glance. It wasn't that long ago that we were saying how we couldn't imagine ever going out as two couples, and here we are—although it didn't happen quite how we imagined!

"Come on," I say. "In we go."

We're shown to a reserved table by the window, take our seats, and start looking at the menus. I know Arthur has no idea what he's looking at, but he seems to enjoy studying the variety of dishes. When Christian suggests a set meal, we're happy to comply, and the waiter goes off with our order.

"So..." Imogen smiles at us. "What have you two been up to today?"

"Arthur's been working." I tell them a little about Max's idea to train him up.

"Immi said you've come to stay for a while," Christian says. "So where are you from, Arthur?"

"New Zealand," Arthur replies.

"Oh, whereabouts? I've got family over there," Christian states.

"A small town on the west coast of the South Island," Arthur says. "Long way from anywhere."

"What did you do over there?"

"This and that." Arthur studies his chopsticks with interest. "Do we eat with these?"

Of course; I'd forgotten about those. Christian gives him a curious look. I just smile. "You can, although we can ask for cutlery if you'd rather."

"No, no, I'll give it a go." He watches me move them up and down, and practices, trying to work out how to organize his fingers.

"Your town isolated, was it?" Christian says.

"I'm a bit of a country bumpkin," Arthur replies. "I haven't travelled much. I apologize if I sound parochial."

"Of course not." Christian is immediately dismissive of the notion. "Life would be dull if we were all the same."

"Absolutely." Imogen is pleased at his kindness, I can tell. "Anyway, what about you, Gwen? What have you been up to?"

"I went out with Una and Duncan to help excavate a Romano-British urn full of coins."

She glances at Arthur, obviously guessing it's something to do with him, but doesn't let on. "Spending a morning on your knees covered in mud and handling thousand-year-old pots? Sounds like your ideal day."

I laugh. "It was, a bit. What about you, how's your day been?"

"Well…" She pauses as the waiter returns with our drinks. She picks up her glass of wine and sips it, waiting until he's left the table. "We got the report back from the coroner," she reveals once we're alone.

"Oh… and?"

"Obviously, this isn't supposed to go any further… blah, blah." She's normally very tight-lipped when it comes to revealing details about cases, but I guess this will become common knowledge soon. "You're not going to believe this. The cause of death was poisoning."

My jaw drops, and the guys' eyebrows rise. "Seriously?" I say.

"Valerie died from an overdose of a chemical called… um… I've forgotten. It's found in some plants and is highly poisonous."

"Digoxin?" I say.

"Yes, that's it."

"It's from foxgloves," I say.

"Right. Apparently, it was used to treat heart failure. Doctors now recommend a combination of ACE inhibitors, beta blockers and…" She screws up her nose as she tries to remember. "…mineralocorti-something antagonists, whatever they are. This drug is apparently a third-line therapy because it increases the risk of death. Anyway, I spoke to her doctor, and he didn't prescribe it because she didn't have heart failure."

"Goodness. How odd."

"So you think someone might have poisoned her with foxgloves?" Arthur asks.

"Possibly," Imogen says.

"They can be found anywhere," I say. "In gardens, woodlands, by the coast, on the side of the road… It's going to be tough isolating where they came from, if that is what killed her. The flowers are only visible from June to September, but all parts of the plant are poisonous, so that doesn't really matter."

"Of course," Christian says, "I forgot that you'd know all about herbs and plants, being a witch." He stops then and looks at Arthur in alarm.

"It's all right," I say, amused. "Arthur knows all about me."

"Double, double, toil and trouble," Arthur says.

That makes me laugh. "I can see which Shakespeare play you've been reading."

"He certainly had a handle on murder," Arthur replies.

"Enough about morbid subjects," Imogen scolds. "We're supposed to be enjoying ourselves."

"I am enjoying myself," Arthur says. "I don't care what we talk about."

"He's easily pleased," I tell her.

"Is he, now?" Her eyes gleam as she sips her wine, and Arthur chuckles.

"Don't be wicked," I scold.

"We like being wicked," Imogen says. "We all enjoy watching you blush."

Chapter Sixteen

Arthur loves Chinese food.

Why am I surprised? I don't think I've found a single thing yet that he doesn't like.

We make our way through a platter of won tons, spring rolls, and pan-fried dumplings, then move on to chicken with cashew nuts, crispy beef, sweet and sour pork, and spicy garlic lamb, with an abundance of noodles and rice.

Arthur masters the chopsticks better than I can. I'm amazed at the ease with which he fits into today's society. I don't think I'd have been half as flexible as he is.

We talk about all sorts of things while we eat, and I'm pleased that Imogen seems relaxed. It's not her first date with Christian, but it's very early on in both our relationships, and yet we all get on better than I think either of us had hoped.

We talk a little about our jobs; Christian tells Arthur what it's like to work as an exhibitions director, and explains how he liaises with the field unit to make sure he always has up-to-date local displays to illustrate current work in the area. We tell him about the urn full of coins that we found, and he promises to talk to Una and Duncan about displaying some of their photos.

"Will the museum put in a bid for the coins, if the coroner classes them as treasure?" I ask.

"It depends on how much they're worth," he says. "If it turns out to be a super-valuable hoard, the British Museum will probably be the only museum who can afford to buy them. If it's of moderate value, we might stand a chance." He twirls his chopsticks in a pile of noodles. "Did you hear they've replaced Liza?"

My eyebrows rise. Liza had just been promoted head of the field unit when she was murdered. "They've not promoted Duncan or Una?" I ask.

He shakes his head. "They've brought in a guy called Kit Vinson. He worked in Oxford and has just moved to the area because his wife got a job teaching at the high school. He seems like a nice guy, quite ambitious. He's hoping to enlarge the field unit and make it more of a player on the national stage."

"That sounds exciting."

He nods. "It's a shame Liza couldn't have done it, but…" He trails off and shrugs, concentrating on his meal.

I meet Imogen's eyes, and she gives a little smile. Christian worked closely with Liza, and he had no idea of the problems I'd had in the past with her. It doesn't sound like Imogen's enlightened him yet, either.

"At least Mary's behind bars," Imogen says, helping herself to more sweet and sour pork.

"I still can't believe she had a thing for you," I say to Christian. "I assumed her motive was to do with her father; I didn't realize it was love."

Christian stops with his chopsticks halfway to his mouth. "What?"

My gaze slides back to Imogen. She gives me a wry look. "I haven't told him about that yet," she advises.

I swear under my breath. "I'm so sorry."

Christian looks confused. "What did you mean?"

"Mary revealed that the reason she murdered Liza was because she thought Liza was having an affair with you," Imogen announces. "Mary had feelings for you—very strong ones, apparently."

Christian blinks. "Wow. I had no idea." He pulls an eek face. "I'm not sure how to feel about that."

"You're like a siren," I tell him, "luring unsuspecting women onto the rocks."

"Don't make me laugh," he says, trying not to smile as we all chuckle. "I feel terrible."

"You shouldn't," Imogen says in her matter-of-fact manner. "Mary has a screw loose. We can't control how other people think, and you can't control how gorgeous you are." She stops then and goes completely scarlet.

I try not to laugh, but I'm on my second glass of sparkling wine, and the giggles rise within me like the bubbles in the glass. Imogen glares at me, but now Arthur and Christian are laughing, and in the end she gives in and smiles as she tries to fan her face with the drinks menu.

"Change the subject," she begs, "please."

So Arthur, bless him, asks Christian what football team he supports, and Christian starts talking about Bristol City F.C., and as soon as Christian discovers that Arthur's never been to a match, he promises to take him, and the conversation moves on.

We finish our meal, then decide to walk down to The Lady of the Lake for a final drink. I've had two big glasses of wine, so I shouldn't have any more, but I don't want the evening to end. It's lovely to have a partner for once, and I know Imogen's feeling the same. So we pay the bill, then—Imogen hand-in-hand with Christian, and me with Arthur—we wander slowly down the road.

It's a cool night, and the stars are out. My fingers intertwine with Arthur's as we walk. I feel happier than I've felt for a long time. I don't want to stop feeling like this. I tighten my hand on Arthur's. I hope he doesn't disappear. Life wouldn't be that cruel, surely?

We arrive at the pub and go inside. Shane Freeman, the owner, has lit a real fire, and the place is busy and warm. We go up to the bar, and Arthur studies the array of bottles with fascination.

"You want to try something different?" I ask.

Christian gestures at the whiskies. "You want a Scotch?"

"Please," Arthur says.

"Do you like Scotch?" I murmur as Christian orders Imogen and I wine, and two glasses of a peaty Islay malt. "That stuff smells like iodine."

"No idea," he admits. "I'll give it a try."

Shane brings over the wine and smiles at us. "Hey, Gwen. Immi."

"Hey." As I smile and take the wine, my gaze wanders to the large mirrors behind him. It takes me a moment to register what I'm seeing.

Behind me, at a table in the window, sit five women. I blink and frown. I know them all. Fenella Davies leans on the table, sipping a glass of red wine. Nancy Armstrong is next to her. Leah Perry sits opposite them, crunching a crisp from a packet.

But it's the other two women who make my jaw drop. One is Mary Paxton, who murdered Liza Banks and who is supposed to be in prison.

The other is Valerie Hopkins-Brown.

I spin around, slopping a little of the wine from the glass onto my hand, and stare at the table. The five women aren't there. It's occupied by a young couple, sitting side-by-side on the seat. He's nuzzling her neck, and she's giggling and blushing.

"Gwen?" Arthur says. "Are you all right?"

I turn back to the bar and look at the mirror. I can still see the five women there, but now I realize that behind them it's daylight, not night-time. I'm not seeing a reflection of the present scene. I'm looking into the past.

Then I blink again, and it's gone.

"Gwen?" It's Imogen's turn to be concerned. "What's the matter?"

I clear my throat. "Can we sit somewhere?"

"Of course." Imogen leads the way to a table not far from the fire. I sink onto the padded seat gratefully.

"Everything all right?" Christian asks, placing his and Arthur's drinks on the table as he sits.

Arthur takes the chair beside him, picks up my hand, and rubs it. "You've gone white as milk," he says.

"I'm sorry." I have a big mouthful of wine. "I've been having visions lately," I explain to Imogen and Christian. "And just then, I saw a scene in the mirror." I explain who I saw and watch Imogen's eyebrows rise.

"Mary was there?" She leans back in her chair and gives a short laugh.

"I don't get it," Christian says.

"We knew that Valerie met with her friends a few days before she died," Imogen replies. "And we knew that Fenella, Leah, and Nancy were there. But we didn't know that Mary was."

"I wonder whether Mary has a tattoo of a triquetra on her wrist," Arthur says.

Imogen and I both stare at him. "Of course," Imogen says softly. "We know Mary is a witch. Maybe they're all part of the same group or something."

"Coven," I say. "They probably belong to the same coven. And the day they met here was Saturday—they were probably celebrating the festival of Ostara."

"Do you belong to a coven?" Christian asks me.

I shake my head. "I'm a kitchen witch, sometimes called a hedge witch or a green witch. I practice alone, doing spells mainly with my baking. But covens are relatively common. I know of at least three here in Glastonbury, and this would make a fourth."

"I never realized. I—" Christian's words are interrupted by Arthur, who has taken a mouthful of whisky and promptly has a fit of coughing.

"I'm okay." His voice comes out as a wheeze. "I'm sorry. I didn't expect that. That's strong stuff."

Christian grins, but gives him a curious look over the top of his rectangular glasses. "You've truly never had whisky?"

"No. Mead was the strongest thing I've drunk." Arthur looks into his glass doubtfully. "I'm not sure this is for me."

"Mead?" Christian laughs. "Where are you from, really? Don't tell me New Zealand. They have whisky there! Anyway, your accent isn't a Kiwi one. You don't drive. You've never even seen chopsticks." He sees Imogen and I exchange a glance, and says, "Come on, guys, you can trust me. I'm not going to go and blab it out to everyone."

Arthur leans his elbows on the table, and the two men study each other for a moment. Arthur's gaze slides to me, then back to Christian. He looks amused rather than angry, but he doesn't speak.

"I'm your friend," Christian says. "Aren't I?"

That makes Arthur smile. "Of course. I'm not being obtuse. My situation is… unusual, that's all."

"What he means," Imogen adds, "is that he's worried you're going to think we're all bonkers and run off and leave me."

"That too," Arthur says.

"I think I'm quickly coming to understand there are a lot of unusual things going on in Glastonbury at the moment," Christian replies. He looks at Imogen, and the softness returns to his eyes that only appears when he looks at her. "And nothing you could say could scare me off."

"I sincerely doubt that," she says.

He grins, then looks back at Arthur. "So come on, then. Are you from a remote tribe in the Amazon rainforest or something?"

"Not quite," Arthur says. "I'm Romano-British."

Christian blinks. "Pardon?"

Arthur runs his hand through his hair and looks at me. "Help?"

"He's sort of a time traveller," I announce.

"Okay…" Christian draws out the word, and I can see his brain struggling to accept this new information.

I look at Imogen, who gives a little shrug. "He's King Arthur," she says. "His spirit was captured in a ruby that was in the pommel of the sword held by Sir Boss in the Avalon Café. Gwen let him out, and here he is."

Christian stares at her. His gaze slides to me. I smile. Then he looks at Arthur.

"King Arthur," he says.

"I was never a king," Arthur states. "But yes, Imogen's telling the truth."

His jaw drops. "You're serious."

It's only now that Imogen's said it out loud that I realize how unbelievable it sounds. But you can't put toothpaste back in the tube.

"I know it sounds incredible," I tell Christian.

"It does. Have you told anyone else?"

"Only Beatrix and Max."

"Shouldn't you tell everyone? Doesn't the world deserve to know?"

"That's up to Arthur," I say. "For a start, nobody would believe him. And if they did, can you imagine what would happen if scientists realized this kind of thing is possible? They'd take him away, lock him up, and do tests on him."

"I don't fancy that," Arthur says.

Christian's lips curve up. "Fair enough." He leans back, accepting the glass of whisky from Arthur as he pushes it across, and he tips the contents into his own glass. "It does explain why you seem... different."

Arthur grins. "I'll take that as a compliment."

I catch Imogen's gaze. I'm surprised she told Christian everything. I would've thought she'd be too afraid that he'd laugh in her face. But I know her well enough to understand she doesn't want secrets between them. She's told him the truth, and if he chooses not to believe it, and to walk away from her because of it, then she'll tell herself she didn't want him in the first place.

She gives me a small smile and turns her gaze to him. "So... you still want to carry on seeing me?"

He looks at her for a long moment. Slowly, he lifts a hand and slips it beneath her hair to the nape of her neck. He pulls her toward him. Eternally recalcitrant, she resists, and he laughs and leans forward, meeting her halfway, and presses his lips to hers.

I watch him kiss her, then drop my gaze because it feels as if I'm prying. I glance at Arthur, who's watching me, a small smile on his lips. His gaze rests on my mouth. He's thinking about kissing me, too.

"I'll get you another drink," I tell him, my voice a squeak, and rise to go to the bar.

I've told him I need time before we let our relationship develop, and that's still true. He needs time to explore his new world and work out exactly what he wants, and I need time to get to know him, and to understand what's happened, and what's going on between us.

So it's good that we haven't kissed yet. Really good. It makes perfect sense.

Groaning, I lean forward and bang my head on the wooden bar.

Chapter Seventeen

About an hour later, we finally decide it's time to go home. Imogen has to work early tomorrow, and I'm tired and know I'll fall asleep as soon as my head hits the pillow.

The two guys are reluctant to leave, though. As soon as Christian accepted that Arthur is who he says he is, he didn't stop asking questions, about what life was like in post-Roman Britain—the buildings, people, clothing, food...

Arthur, being Arthur and completely understanding someone's fascination with information and knowledge, answered every question Christian could come up with and more, and I can see that he loves Christian's deep understanding of not just the Dark Ages, but of history in general.

Christian promises to take Arthur to football and fishing with him. Arthur agrees to spend some time at the museum, discussing possible new exhibitions. I know Imogen is as delighted as I am that the two of them appear to have struck up a firm friendship.

We part at the top of the hill, shaking hands and giving hugs, and Imogen winks at me before the two of them head off. Is she taking him back to her place? I hope so. She hasn't dated for several years after a previous relationship ended badly. She's thrown herself into her work, and she definitely deserves some fun.

Arthur and I walk slowly back to the house. It's cool now, and I'm glad of his hand warming mine. I glance up at him, feeling a strange sense of awe as I remind myself who he is. He's so handsome. Will I really be lucky enough to keep this guy all to myself?

"The stars are bright tonight," I say, to cover the unease that refuses to go away.

"They are." He stops and looks up at them. "They're one thing that's stayed the same, which is reassuring." Raising an arm, he traces Ursa Major, also called the Plough or, as my mum used to call it, the

Saucepan. "I'll have to do some reading about astronomy. Apparently there's a telescope in space that takes photos of the stars."

"Yes, the Hubble. The pictures of galaxies are amazing."

He shakes his head. "It's a wonderful world."

I smile. "It's so lovely to hear someone say that. You'd be surprised how many people fail to appreciate the fantastic advances we've made."

He holds my hand again, and we continue walking. "I grew up in the years after the Romans had left Britain," he says. "For a while, life carried on as it always had, but without that connection with Rome, everything gradually crumbled. People began leaving the cities. The roads became overgrown. The hypocaust systems stopped working, and the aqueducts fell into disrepair. The brilliance of Rome was still in living memory, so we knew what we were missing, and we longed for it. Maybe that's why I have a greater appreciation."

"Maybe. Or perhaps your mind is just more expansive." I squeeze his fingers. "It was odd watching Christian with you. He's highly intelligent, and he doesn't suffer fools gladly. He can be impatient when someone doesn't understand the point he's trying to get across. But even though you didn't know how to use chopsticks, and you'd never had whisky, he found you fascinating because you have a thirst for knowledge, and you're not afraid to say 'I don't know, tell me how that works.'"

Arthur smiles at me. "I'm glad you find it an attractive thing. I'll be saying 'I don't know' an awful lot."

We both chuckle, and then he holds open the front garden gate for me. I go up the garden path and open the door with my key.

We go into the living room and discover Merlin lying in front of the fire. He lifts his head as we walk in and wags his tail.

"It's all right," Arthur says, "don't get up."

I laugh. "Well, I think I might go to bed. I'm very tired."

"Of course. Sleep well."

"Are you staying up?"

"I might have a read for a while," he says.

I meet his eyes. His lips curve up a little. I think he's thinking about kissing me again, but I know he's not going to.

"Thank you for a lovely evening," I say softly.

"Thank you for inviting me out with your friends. I had a great time. Immi's lovely, and I enjoyed Christian's company." He grins. "I thought he reacted very well to the revelation."

"Much better than I'd hoped," I admit. "We shouldn't tell anyone else, though. I'm worried that if it gets out…" I hesitate, not sure how to put my fears into words.

"I know," he murmurs. "And I'll say it again. I'm not going anywhere, Gwen."

His words reassure me a little. And I like the way he says my name. It gives me goose bumps.

"All right. I'll see you tomorrow."

"Goodnight."

I leave him with Merlin, and go upstairs.

When I'm in bed, I lie there for a while and think about the evening. I'm lucky enough to have a lot of friends. I often meet up with people for coffee or a drink in the evenings, and I have Beatrix and Delia as mother figures. And I've known Imogen forever. But for the first time, I feel as if I have people of my own. This thing with Imogen and Christian is going to be lasting—I can feel it. He knows the truth about Arthur, and he didn't mock us or back away in horror. He's going to be there for Arthur, just like Max, which is important, because no matter how strong Arthur is, how solid, he's in a very strange situation, and he's going to need support at times.

And the promise of our relationship lies on the horizon like a Fata Morgana—a mirage that just might turn out to be real.

I close my eyes, my lips curved up in a smile, and within moments I fall asleep.

*

In the morning, I get up, shower and dress, and go downstairs to discover the house empty. Puzzled, I walk into the kitchen and discover a note on the table. It's the first time I've seen Arthur's handwriting—it looks like something a medieval monk would have written in a beautiful script; it must have taken him ages. Laughing, I open the note. It says, "Gwen—I'm trying jogging. Back soon." He's signed it with an elaborate X.

Jogging? Grinning, I put on some toast and start making coffee. By the time it's ready, I hear the front door opening, and then Merlin comes in, followed by Arthur.

Merlin's panting, and he immediately lies down on the tiles. Arthur laughs. "He says I'm going to kill him. He's not very fit."

He's wearing a pair of jogging bottoms and a grey T-shirt that has a deep V of sweat on the front. Sweat also glistens on his brow and in the hollow at the base of his throat. My knees feel a little weak.

"Good morning," he says, smiling. "You look lovely today."

I'm wearing jeans and a white shirt ready for work, and I've knotted my hair up in its usual scruffy bun, so I'm nothing special, but I glow inside at the admiration on his face.

"Sweet talker," I tell him. "How was your run?"

"Exhilarating. I like jogging. It was good to stretch my legs." He takes his phone out of his pocket. "I saw other joggers with little things in their ears."

"Headphones?"

"Is that what they were?"

"They were probably listening to music. Or possibly audio books. That's someone reading out stories."

Arthur's eyebrows rise. "There is such a thing? And music..." He leans on the back of one of the kitchen chairs. "I used to listen to the radio in the café. I liked some of the music on there."

"I'll download Spotify for your phone," I tell him. "Then you'll be able to listen to any song you like."

"Please," he says, and hands the phone to me.

I take it, but hesitate. "Are you sure you don't mind me looking at it?"

"Why would I?"

"I don't know... privacy is an important thing nowadays. Everyone has a password on their phone to stop others looking. I don't want you to think I'm invading your privacy."

He gives a short laugh. Then he comes around the table to stand in front of me. He bends his head. And then he kisses me on the forehead. "You're very sweet," he says. Then he turns, leaves the room, and goes up the stairs, saying, "I'll have a shower."

I smile and open my mouth to reply. At that moment, I look up at the glass door of the cupboard in front of me. A figure is standing behind me. She's wearing a white dress and carrying flowers, and her long brown hair hangs down around her waist. It's Valerie.

I inhale sharply, and beside me Merlin stiffens. My heart races at a million miles an hour, banging on my ribs. I look behind me, but there's no ghost, no sign of the dead woman. And when I look back at the glass door, she's gone.

"I suppose I'm going to have to get used to this," I say to Merlin. "This will probably keep happening until we solve her murder. That's an incentive to get to work, if ever I've heard one."

*

Arthur comes with me to the café, declaring that there must be something he can do to help there.

"I do have several odd jobs, if you're in the mood," I say as we pull up.

"Absolutely. Just point me in the right direction."

We go into the café. Delia's there, and so is Melissa, her sister.

"We weren't sure whether you were coming in," Delia states once we've said good morning.

"I'm happy to go if you want me to," Melissa adds.

"No, please stay, if you're not busy," I tell her. "I'll work for a bit, but I might go out again later."

"Of course," Delia says. She pauses for a moment, but I can see she's thinking about whether to say something else. I give her a smile of encouragement. "I was wondering…" she begins.

"Yes?"

She looks around the café. It's early, so there's only one person having a coffee at a table the moment, but she still gestures with her head toward the corridor at the back. Leaving Arthur talking to Cooper, I follow her, and she glances through the window at the kitchen, where Allison and Joss have just arrived and are putting on their aprons, ready to start making sandwiches and rolls. Delia turns into the break room instead, and when I follow her in, she closes the door behind me.

"What's up?" I ask. She doesn't look upset, just a little nervous.

"I've been thinking," she says. "About your baking."

"Yes…"

She takes a deep breath. "I wondered whether you'd be willing to show me a few of the… recipes you use." Her eyes meet mine.

I frown. "They're all in the folder in the kitchen. You know that."

"Yes… well, I didn't mean recipes… I meant… spells."

I stare at her for a long moment. I've never told her that I'm a witch, and she's never mentioned it. I wasn't aware she knew there was anything different about my baking.

"Oh," I say. "Goodness."

She clenches her hands in front of her, clearly worried she's overstepped the mark. "I'm so sorry. If you don't want to talk about it, I'll never mention it again. But I worked with your mother for some years, and then with you, and I know there's something special about how you bake. I know you do something with the herbs you use. I don't know how, but I can… feel it." She reddens.

I'm so surprised, I'm not sure what to say.

"I'd love to learn," she says softly. "I've always been interested in witchcraft, but my mother would never have allowed me to study it, and I've never met anyone else who's interested. Would you teach me?"

Pleasure floods me, and I catch her hands in mine. "Of course I will. Oh, I wish I'd known this years ago!"

She laughs and puts her arms around me, and we exchange a big hug.

"I just thought that if I could help you," she says, "it would mean that maybe you could take some more time off to be with Arthur." She smiles. "He seems like a lovely young man."

It's my turn to blush. "He is. And I think that's a wonderful idea." It flashes through my mind that Duncan and Una asked if I'd like to help with sorting through the coins from the urn. It might mean I can help out at the field unit a bit more, especially now Liza's gone. I never wished her harm, but I could never have gone there while she was alive.

"I'll get the morning's baking done," I say, "and then we'll have a chat, okay? Witchcraft 101."

"I look forward to it." She looks genuinely thrilled as we leave the room.

I collect Arthur, explain where our tool bag is kept, and show him the few jobs that need doing. One of the tables has a wobbly leg. The hinge on the door to the kitchen is squeaky. In the breakroom, we could really do with a couple of shelves above the sink.

"This room could do with a splash of paint," Arthur says, glancing around.

"That would be wonderful," I say with enthusiasm. "I've thought it for a while, but I never have the time to do it."

"Leave it with me," he says, and goes off to get the tool bag.

I go into the kitchen and take down the big ceramic mixing bowl that was my grandmother's, and smile as I begin the process of making the day's muffins.

Chapter Eighteen

I bake all morning, until the shelves are stocked with muffins, sausage rolls, and fresh cakes, most of which contain specially prepared herbs and a touch of magic. While I work, I see Arthur occasionally, walking about with screwdrivers and hammers, and soon the squeaky door and the wobbly table are fixed, and then I hear the sound of the drill in the break room, so I know he's putting up the shelves.

Then I do as I promised and sit with Delia in the corner of the café while we talk.

As it's only our first conversation, I keep it light and go through the principles of blessing herbs and spices. I explain how the rhymes a witch says as she does her spells are less important than the intention behind them. To illustrate, I use my recipe for my savoury energy muffins, and illustrate how I bless the chilli flakes and other spices with a short spell while I imagine the consumer being filled with energy and light.

"A lot of the recipes come from my mother, grandmother, and great-grandmother," I say. "But I've made a lot more of my own. The recipe book in the kitchen is really a family Book of Shadows."

"Your mum was very careful with her witchcraft," Delia says. "I walked into the kitchen once when she was halfway through reciting a spell. She got very embarrassed and just walked out. I never felt as able to talk to her as I do to you."

"Mum was a very private person," I concede. "I don't know whether that was connected to her illness, or if she'd always been that way. I mean, don't get me wrong, we were very close, and she taught me almost everything I know about witchcraft. But her lessons were always very... structured, I suppose. Grandma was much more open."

"I wish I'd met Lizzie," Delia says. "I think I would've liked her from what people have told me about her."

"Oh everyone did. She was very warm and friendly." I sip the coffee that Cooper made me and sigh. "I think Mum might have been very different if Dad hadn't died when I was young. She had so many years on her own. I think she was lonely." I study the cup in my hands. "I was worried I might end up like her. Is that a terrible thing to say?"

"I think it would be a very normal worry," Delia replies gently. "But I can't see you ending up alone, Gwen. Especially now a certain young man has turned up." Her eyes twinkle.

I chuckle. "I think he would be thrilled to hear himself described as a young man, especially by you. You're only in your forties!"

"I know. I feel older." She grins. "He did seem very taken with you. How long have you known him?"

"Oh, most of my life." Arthur and I have prepared the background story. "He's a distant cousin I knew as a child. We kept in touch after he moved to New Zealand, and when he said he was coming back for a visit, I said he was welcome to stay with me."

"Well he certainly couldn't take his eyes off you when you were together." She smiles. "I'm pleased for you. You work so hard, and you deserve to have some fun."

"Talking of which," I say, finishing off my coffee, "I think I'll take a few hours off, if you're okay here."

"Of course. You've done amazing this morning. Melissa's here, and Cooper's not going into college today. We'll cover the shop."

I give her a hug, collect my jacket and handbag, and go and see Arthur, who's in the process of finishing off the final shelf.

"They look great," I say enthusiastically. "You mastered the drill, then?"

"What an amazing piece of machinery." He steps back and admires his handiwork. "We could have done with one of those when we were putting up our houses."

I smile. "Do you fancy a break?"

He washes his hands in the sink. "What did you have in mind?"

"I thought we'd do some more investigating, starting with Fenella's place."

"Sounds fun," he says, drying his hands, then picking up his jacket. "Come on, then."

We wave goodbye to everyone in the café. Then, collecting Merlin from out the front of the café on the way, we head over to the car.

"Merlin wants to know where we're going," Arthur says as we get in. He grins. He knows Merlin didn't like it there.

"We're going to Dogs All Day," I say as I take the road south toward The Roman Way. I glance in my rear-view mirror. Somehow, the dog manages to look alarmed. "I'm not leaving you there," I tell him, amused.

"I understand his reticence," Arthur says. "They weren't a particularly likeable family."

"I know. But I've been thinking about what Imogen told us yesterday, about Valerie being poisoned by the substance that comes from foxgloves. I'm going to pay her three friends a visit and see if any of them have foxgloves in their gardens."

"Maybe that's what poisoned the Spaniel," Arthur suggests.

"It's very possible—it's toxic to both humans and animals. We'll have a hunt around and see if we can find any."

It's not long before I'm taking the turn-off onto the drive for the kennels. I pass through the line of beech trees, and park in the same place as last time, in front of the manor house.

I turn the engine off and we both look over our shoulders. The dog looks back at us, distinctly unimpressed.

"Come on," I tell him, trying not to laugh. "I promise not to let you out of my sight."

We get out, I clip the leash on his collar, and we start walking toward the kennels. As we approach, Fenella comes out.

"Good morning!" She strides up to us. "Nice to see you here again."

Arthur and I shake her hand. "I hope you don't mind me calling in," I say.

"Not at all. How can I help?"

"I wanted to check your calendar and see if I can book Merlin in for next month," I tell her. "And then I wondered whether I could be cheeky enough to have a little walk around the kennels and gardens with him, to try to get him used to the place?"

"He does look rather nervous," she says.

"He's a rescue dog," Arthur says, which is partly the truth. "He appeared on Gwen's doorstep six months ago, so we're not sure what kind of socializing he's had growing up."

"Aw," she says, "poor thing. Yes, have a look around the kennels and the garden. Take your time. When you're done, knock on the back door of the house and I'll double check the calendar."

"Thank you so much," I say, "I really appreciate it. I just want him to be happy."

"Yes, of course," she replies, in a voice that suggests she's thinking *He's only a dog.*

"Okay. Come on then, boy." We take the path around the kennels, Merlin trotting beside us.

We walk slowly around the buildings, taking our time in the beautiful spring afternoon. "Do you know why foxgloves are so called?" I ask Arthur. "They were first mentioned in 1542 by a man called Leonhard Fuchs, which is German for fox. It's also where fuchsia comes from. Anyway, the genus is called digitalis from the Latin for finger, probably because the flowers are a finger's length when they're fully grown."

"How interesting."

"I knew you'd appreciate it," I tell him. "At long last, someone who likes useless facts as much as I do."

He chuckles as we leave the kennels behind us and head around the edge of the large lawn. Part of it is fenced off, and six dogs are out playing in the pen, chasing balls and sniffing around the base of the apple tree inside it. There are no flowers inside the pen, though, and no borders around the edge of the lawn.

As I near the left-hand side of the garden, however, on the other side of the house, I see there's a gate in a high fence dividing the main lawn from a smaller, more private garden. Arthur sees it too, and, making sure we're not being watched, he holds open the gate, and we go through.

I would have said it was an attempt to cultivate an English country garden, but I think that actually it's just been left to go wild. There are weeds in the borders and the lawn is knee-high. It's beautiful, though, full of butterflies, from white Brimstones to Red Admirals to a beautiful Painted Lady.

They flutter around the wide array of flowers, and I hum the words from the old song *English Country Garden* as I spot pansies, grape hyacinths, crocuses, late daffodils, azaleas, and hellebores. It's too early for foxgloves to flower, so I'm not expecting to see the purple-pink spikes anywhere.

And then, by a wall, I spot a patch of tall green stems with distinctive leaves.

"Look," I say, pointing. "They're foxgloves."

"Don't touch anything," Arthur warns Merlin. Obediently, he sits on the path, letting me approach the patch of light-green stalks.

"They're definitely foxgloves. And it doesn't matter that they haven't flowered, as the stalks and leaves are also poisonous."

"Could they have caused the death of the Spaniel?" Arthur asks.

I frown. "I don't know. The gate was securely fastened, and it doesn't look as if the dogs are allowed out of the pen anyway. He would need to have crossed the lawn, got through the gate and into the garden, found the foxgloves, and then eaten them, which seems like a stretch."

"But they could have caused Valerie's death," Arthur says.

"Yes, definitely."

"Do you want to take a sample?"

"No, I don't want to touch them. Let's leave. I want to get Merlin out."

"All right." Arthur leads the way out of the garden, and I make sure I wait until Merlin's followed him. He might have the soul of a man, but he's still a dog at heart, and the last thing I'd want is for him to accidentally eat some.

When we're out, we exit the garden at the front of the house and cross to the car. We've just reached it when Fenella comes running out, waving a hand. "Don't you want to go through the calendar?" she calls.

"Sorry," I yell back, "I've just had an important phone call, and there's an emergency at the café. I've got to go. I'll call you later." I open the back door to let Merlin in, and then we get in and drive off.

"My heart's racing," I announce, blowing out a breath.

"So Fenella's definitely on our list of suspects, then?" Arthur says.

"I would say so, wouldn't you?" My mind churns furiously as I drive. "Maybe she did kill the Spaniel. Perhaps she ground up the foxglove and put it in his food. And she could have done the same to Valerie."

"Are we still going to check out the others?"

"Oh yes. The foxglove is relatively common around here. We need to see whether the other two have it in their gardens."

I turn left at the roundabout. "So we need to work out where Nancy Armstrong lives. Can you Google the BT phone book? You should be able to look her up."

He pulls out his phone and types the website with one finger. King Arthur using a mobile phone. It makes me smile.

"She's not on here," he says. "Maybe you could ask James Mackenzie at the jewellery shop?"

"How can I do that without Nancy being there?"

"Didn't she say she worked at the abbey on Tuesday and Thursday afternoons with the Living History group?"

"She did! Well remembered." I drive past the Avalon Café, turn right into the high street, and park near to the jewellery shop. "You can stay here if you like," I tell Merlin, and he flops down on the seat and immediately begins snoring.

Chuckling, we get out and walk down to Mackenzie's. Inside, it's relatively quiet, with just one woman buying a pair of earrings. James finishes serving her, and then turns to us with a smile.

"Gwen! Arthur! How are you?"

"Good, thank you," I reply. "I won't keep you long. I was just wondering whether you would be able to tell me where Nancy lived. I found a book on medieval costumes in the loft, and I thought she might like it for inspiration for her Living History. You know, to cheer her up."

"How thoughtful of you. Yes, of course, she's out at South Wick Hollow. Number twenty-one. You'll recognize the house from all the beehives."

I stare at him in surprise. "I presume you're not referring to the hairdo."

He laughs. "No, she keeps bees. Mind you don't get stung!"

"I will, thanks, James. How are you…" My voice trails off. Next to him, on the wall, is a large clock. The centre of it is a mirror, and in the reflection, standing behind me is a woman in white.

I spin around, but of course she's not there, and when I look back at the clock, she's gone.

"Gwen?" James looks concerned. "Are you all right?"

Arthur looks at the clock, then frowns at me.

"Sorry," I say, aware my voice holds a little wobble. "Something buzzed by my ear. I think it was the talk of the bees."

Arthur smiles at James. "Thanks for your help. See you later."

Holding my hand, he takes me outside to the car.

"What happened?" he asks once we're inside.

"I saw Valerie's ghost again." I start the engine, then blow out a breath. "I need to get used to seeing spirits, because I don't think it's going to stop anytime soon." I steer the car out and head for home.

"I'm going to pick up a book from home that I can take to her house. That was interesting though, wasn't it? What do you think about Nancy keeping bees?"

"Maybe Valerie was allergic to bee stings?"

"Hmm. Maybe. I guess the coroner would have picked that up, but it's worth keeping in mind."

Chapter Nineteen

We call home and pick up the book, then drive a little way out of town, along the route we took when we went to find Arthur's coins, and soon come to twenty-one South Wick Hollow. I park out the front, hoping Nancy isn't in, although that's why I brought the book, just in case. This time, we make Merlin stay in the car.

The house is small but nicely kept, the wooden window frames freshly painted white, the borders weeded, and the lawn free of leaves from the surrounding hedges. We go through the wrought-iron gate and up to the front door, and I knock, crossing my fingers that she's not in. Luckily, there's no reply.

"Right." I turn and lead the way across the lawn, examining the borders as I go. There are sunshine-yellow crocuses, forget-me-nots, columbine, sweet alyssum, and candelabra primroses. Nancy also has borders along the pathway on the side of the house that receives the sun, filled with daffodils, violas, hyacinths, and oleanders just coming into flower. The spread gives an Easter egg effect, all yellows and greens and purples, very pleasing to the eye.

There's no sign of foxgloves, though.

"Bees," Arthur says. "Careful." He's right; as we walk around the house to the back, we start to see honeybees feeding from the flowers. When we reach the lawn, the hives are easily visible at the bottom of the garden, and the air is filled with the light hum of bees at work.

"We'll just take a quick look around the borders," I tell Arthur, leading the way and doing my best not to get flustered as the bees move between the crocuses, calendula, lavender, and wild lilac.

"Fun fact," I tell Arthur. "Bees can't see red."

"Really?"

"I'm not sure how we know that," I admit, "but apparently it's true."

"Can you see any foxgloves?"

"No." I frown as we cut across the lawn to avoid the hives. "No sign yet."

Arthur lifts an arm as a bee lands on his sleeve, and he studies it with interest. "I wonder how many animals and insects that are alive today are different from ones in the sixth century?"

"Not many. The lynx, the wolf, and the brown bear are three that supposedly died out after the Romans left. I'm sure there are insects, but they weren't well documented that far back."

We finish traversing the lawn and arrive at the house. "No foxgloves," I say. "It doesn't clear Nancy, but if it was her, she didn't get the poison from her own garden." I feel a touch of frustration. "Is this pointless? It doesn't really prove anything."

"No, but it's important information," Arthur says. "You can pass it onto Immi, and maybe something you discover will help her decipher the bigger picture."

"I suppose." I smile at him as we return to the front garden. "Well, only one more garden to visit—Leah's."

"I was thinking," Arthur replies, "should we take a look at Valerie's place, too?" He holds open the gate for me.

"You think her husband is a suspect?" I go through.

He closes the gate behind us. "I seem to recall from watching detective shows on the TV in the café that most murders are committed by someone you know."

"That's true. In that case, yes, we should take a look. Oh!" I come to a halt at the sight of Nancy Armstrong walking toward us from where she's obviously just parked her car.

"Hello," she says. "Well this is a surprise. What are you two doing here?" She smiles, but it doesn't seem to reach her eyes. Or am I reading too much, and is she just surprised by our presence?

"I was passing, and thought I'd drop this off." I show her the book in my hand. "I thought you might be able to use it as inspiration for costumes for your Living History group."

She takes it from me. "How thoughtful."

"I felt bad for you," I murmur, "after our conversation about Valerie. You must feel very sad, and I wanted to cheer you up."

"You could have just dropped it off at the jewellery shop," she says. Her eyes meet mine, cautious, shrewd.

"We had it in the car and we were out for a drive," Arthur says. "So we thought we'd drop it in."

"How did you know where I lived?" She looks up and down the road. I'm not sure if she's checking to see if any neighbours are watching, or if she's expecting someone.

"James told us," I say, starting to feel uncomfortable. "I am sorry if you feel it's an intrusion."

Her smile returns. "Not at all, I was surprised, that's all. It was a lovely gesture, thank you."

"Okay, well, we'll be off now." I slide my hand into Arthur's, and we wave goodbye and head back to the car.

"That was close," Arthur says as I pull away. "I got the feeling she didn't believe us."

"Me too." I head back down the country lane, relieved to be away. "I suppose it was a bit odd, dropping the book off. But plausible."

"I thought so." He gives Merlin's head a rub as the dog sticks it between our seats. "Shall I look for Valerie and Leah's addresses?"

"Yes, please. Hopefully they'll be on there this time."

He pulls out his phone and taps the keys carefully. "Success this time," he announces. "Valerie Hopkins-Brown, Windmill Hill Road." He reads out the number.

"That's not far. We'll go there next."

He looks up Leah Perry. "She's here, too. Flat C, 29 Hawkins Terrace."

"A flat?" I frown. "She's unlikely to have a garden, then. But we'll check it out to make sure."

I drive the short distance through the Somerset countryside. The road runs around a central park with a cluster of horse chestnut trees. I pull the car up a few spaces down from Valerie's house, put on the handbrake, and turn off the engine.

I glance in the rear-view mirror, and inhale sharply. On the back seat, next to Merlin, sits the woman in white.

I whip my head around, but only Merlin is there, staring at the space where Valerie was sitting.

"She was here," I tell Arthur. "Sitting right there."

He twists around to look over at the back seat. "Was that a warning? Or just because we're at her house?"

"I don't know." My heart is hammering, but not just because I've seen Valerie's ghost. Arthur is now close to me, the line of his jaw, showing a touch of stubble, only inches away. It would be oh-so-easy to lean forward and press my lips to his, lift his sweater and slide my hands beneath it, onto his warm skin. It's such an overwhelming desire that it shocks me.

His gaze comes back to me, his blue eyes the colour of the spring sky. His gaze drops to my mouth, and I know he's thinking about kissing me, too. I hold my breath as he lowers his head toward me.

A rap on the window makes us both jump, and I spin around, half-expecting to see Valerie outside, cross that we've let ourselves be distracted from solving her murder. But it's not Valerie.

It's Matthew Hopkins.

I grit my teeth. "What does he want?" I open the car door, and Matthew steps back as I get out. Arthur gets out, too, and opens the passenger door. Out of the corner of my eye, I see Merlin jump down and trot off.

"What are you doing here?" Matthew demands.

"Good morning," I say as pleasantly as I can. "How are you?"

His gaze slides to Arthur as he comes around the car to stand beside me. Arthur leans on the car door casually, one hand in his pocket, but he's near enough to me to make his point—Matthew isn't to come any closer.

"I said, what are you doing here?" Matthew repeats.

"We came to pay our respects to Bradley," I reply.

"He doesn't want to see anyone," Matthew states. "So you can go now."

I fold my arms, trying not to let him intimidate me. "I'm surprised to see you here. I didn't think you and Valerie were on speaking terms."

He looks away then, across the park, and he's unable to stop the emotion that flickers on his face. Her death has affected him—of course it has. She was his sister.

I reach out a hand and rest it on his upper arm. "I'm very sorry," I say quietly. "This must be extremely hard for you."

He looks down at my hand. "We hadn't spoken for ten years." His voice is gruff.

"I'm sure that she knew you loved her, despite your differences."

He lifts his gaze back to me. His eyes are dark blue, almost grey, like the colour of a stormy sky. He's a handsome man, but there's something about him that makes my skin crawl. A memory flashes through my mind of the moment when he kissed me, and without thinking, I take a step back.

His brow darkens. "I want you to go," he snaps. "Bradley doesn't want to see anyone."

"That's not for you to say," I reply, but he's growing angry, his hands clenching into fists.

"Just leave," he yells, "or I'll call the police!"

"Come on." Arthur rests a hand on my back. "Let's go."

I'm reluctant, because I haven't yet seen Valerie's garden, and I'm desperate to stop her ghost showing up, but Matthew's menacing expression makes me back away, and I get into the car. Arthur turns as Merlin runs up, and he opens the back door to let the dog jump in before getting in himself. I pull away, leaving Matthew's face in the mirror behind me.

I blow out a long breath. Arthur reaches out and takes my free hand.

"I'm sorry," he says.

"I'm just annoyed that we didn't get a look at the garden," I tell him.

"We did. Merlin ran around it."

I look in my rear-view mirror at the dog, whose tongue lolls out as if he's laughing.

"He says she had foxgloves on one side, by the wall."

"Are you sure?" I ask the dog. "I don't mean to doubt you, but how do you know?"

"As Taliesin, he studied herbs and flowers," Arthur says. "He was a druid, as well as a bard."

My mouth forms an O. "I didn't realize."

"He trained on the Isle of Avalon. There was a school there for both witches and druids. They taught the healing arts, and other disciplines like history, music, and poetry. He's ten times smarter than me." Arthur looks over his shoulder at the dog. "But I have opposable thumbs, so I think that makes me superior."

Merlin snorts and lies down on the back seat, and we both laugh.

"You two," I scold. "But thank you, Merlin, for finding that out for us."

"So Valerie's and Fenella's houses have foxgloves, but Nancy's doesn't," Arthur comments. "I wonder what Leah will have?"

"We'll find out in a minute." I signal to take the turning into town.

It only takes us about five minutes to reach Hawkins Terrace. It's just off the high street, a row of tall terraced houses, many of which have been divided into apartments. Number twenty-nine looks just like the others—the door opens straight onto the road, with no front garden. When we get out and walk down a back alley to peer over the fence, we see that the back yard is mainly concreted with a small lawn, a bench, and an array of pot plants, none of which contain foxgloves.

"So Leah doesn't have them close by either," I say as we get back in the car. "But of course, it doesn't mean she didn't do it. She could easily have picked them wild, or from someone else's garden."

I sigh and start the engine. "It's getting late. Time to go home. I'll call Immi tonight and tell her what we've found out. I can't imagine it'll be much help."

"You never know."

"No." I smile at him. "What would you like for dinner tonight? I'll cook you anything you fancy."

"Pizza," he says. "I've heard so much about it, and I'm desperate to try it."

I laugh. "All right. Pizza it is."

Chapter Twenty

Arthur watches while I make the pizza dough and form it into two circles on baking trays. I add some tomato paste and dried Italian mixed herbs. Then I retrieve a variety of possible toppings from the fridge, and we add what we want to our pizzas.

Arthur tastes everything first, from anchovies and capers to salami and mozzarella cheese. Max was right: he does like meat, and creates his own meat feast pizza with the salami, strips of ham, piles of cooked chicken, and a sliced chorizo sausage. I go more for vegetables with mushrooms, sweetcorn, and onions, and we top both of them with a homemade barbecue sauce. Then we put them in the oven and set the timer.

"So the only thing I've found that you don't like is whisky," I say as I pour kibble into Merlin's bowl and add a raw egg. As a treat, I tip in the leftover chicken, and Merlin does a tap dance on the tiles as I put the dish down.

"It tasted like the earth," Arthur says.

"That's because it was an Islay malt."

"Eye-lah?"

"That's how it's pronounced; it's spelled I-s-l-a-y. It's an island off the west coast of Scotland. The smoky flavour comes from the peat in the area. It's an acquired taste. You might prefer something like a Glenfiddich." I open the cupboard beside the sink and take out a bottle.

I retrieve a tray of ice cubes from the freezer. Arthur watches with fascination as I twist it and tip out two cubes into each glass. "And it stores food, too," he says, looking into the freezer and studying the chicken breasts, packets of mince, and ice cream inside. "How amazing."

"One of mankind's better inventions." I pour some whisky over the ice and add a splash of water. Then I slide a glass over to him. "The

Glenfiddich is more fruity, with a touch of pear, and sweet too, like butterscotch."

He takes a cautious sip. Then another. His eyes meet mine and he runs his tongue over his teeth. "Better than the Islay," he says.

"I think so." I smile. "I'm going to give Immi a quick ring before dinner's ready."

"All right. I'll have a read." Picking up his whisky, he leaves the room.

I watch him walk away, blowing out a breath as I admire his broad shoulders and slim hips before he disappears around the corner, then pick up my phone and dial Imogen's number.

"DCI Hobbs," she answers. She's still at work.

"It's me," I say. "Are you busy?"

"Yes, but I'm happy to take five," she replies. "I'll get a cup of coffee." I hear her move back her chair and imagine her walking out of her office and down to the kitchen in the station. "How are you doing?" she asks.

"Yes, good thanks. Arthur and I have done a little investigating, and I thought I'd pass on what we found out."

"Absolutely. Go for it."

So I summarize the day's events, explaining how we discovered foxgloves in Fenella's and Valerie's gardens, but none in Nancy's, and that Leah lived in a flat. "I know it's not conclusive," I add. "Obviously they could have got them from someone else's garden. But it's a start."

"It is." There are clinking noises as she stirs coffee in a mug, and then footsteps again as she returns to her office. "I'm trying to work out how she imbibed the substance. I presume it was in food or drink. She'd eaten cereal and milk with blueberries and a banana for breakfast that morning, with lemon, ginger, and honey tea. I'm getting everything tested."

"Was the tea in teabags?"

"Yes, and the packet was opened. Maybe the flowers were ground up in there. We'll find out soon. By the way, I found out something else today. I went to see Mary Paxton."

My eyebrows rise. "Why?"

"Instinct. You'll never guess what. She has a triquetra tattoo on her wrist."

That does shock me. "Did you ask her about it?"

"I did, but she refused to talk about it. I've also asked the others, but they're very tight-lipped."

"Hmm."

"I thought maybe you could do some research," she says. "See if you come across anything."

"Of course." I feel pleased that she wants my help. "By the way," I add, "I ran into Matthew Hopkins today. That wasn't pleasant."

"What an obnoxious man. I hope you put him in his place."

"I backed away carefully. Arthur was with me. He doesn't like Matthew."

She laughs. "I'm not surprised. So... how's it going with you two?"

I smile. "Very well."

"He's still staying with you?"

"He is. In the spare room, I feel I should point out."

"It's none of my business," she says. "But tell me everything."

I chuckle. "I told him I need time before we... you know... let our relationship develop. I mean, he's gorgeous, and I really like him, but I've only known him two days!"

"I suppose to him it seems a lot longer."

"Yes, I'm aware of that." I push a small stone on the floor with the toe of my slipper. "Do you think I'm crazy? I know it's not a problem nowadays to sleep with a guy on a first date. We women are supposed to be liberated. But this isn't just a fling, or at least I hope it isn't. I want to do it right."

"Nothing wrong with that," Imogen replies. "He doesn't strike me as the type of guy who'll look elsewhere if you don't fall into bed with him immediately. And if he does, he's not worth it anyway."

"Good point."

"Has he kissed you?"

"Not yet. We've come close a couple of times, but something has always interrupted us."

"Do you want to kiss him?"

"Goddess, yes!"

She laughs at my vehement reply. "It'll happen when it's supposed to. He only has eyes for you, Gwen. Just do what comes naturally, what feels right. It doesn't matter if takes a day, a month, or a year for things to happen, as long as you feel happy and safe and comfortable with him."

I smile, wishing she was here so I could give her a hug. "You're such a sweetie. How about you and Christian? How are things going there?"

"He walked me home last night. We had the best smoochy kiss I've ever had in my life."

I laugh. "I'm so glad to hear that. Where did he kiss you?"

"On the mouth."

"I meant where geographically?"

"Oh, sorry, on the porch. I didn't ask him in. Like you, I don't want to fast track this. But I was tempted. He's a great kisser. He even took off his glasses."

"Wow, that shows dedication."

"Doesn't it?" She sighs. "He was holding my hands at first, and then he lifted a hand to my face and slipped it into my hair... It was pretty damn good."

"I'm so green it's like I'm made of chlorophyll."

She gives a girlish giggle. "Well when your first kiss happens, I expect to hear all about it."

"You'll hear the sirens because I'll have passed out from lack of oxygen," I tell her. "I can barely breathe when I'm sitting a few inches from him in the car, let alone if he were to kiss me."

I look up, and to my shock Arthur's standing in the doorway. He's not looking at me, though, he's waiting for Merlin to follow him, and when he turns, he doesn't give any indication that he heard what I said.

I swallow hard. "Gotta go."

"Oops. Is he there? Did he hear you?"

"Possibly. Speak to you later."

"Good luck!" She hangs up.

I leave the phone on the table and go over to the oven as Arthur lets Merlin into the garden. "Pizzas are nearly done," I call, my voice a squeak.

"They smell amazing." He smiles. Is there a twinkle in his eye or am I imagining it?

But he still doesn't say anything, and I let the moment pass. He retrieves some plates, and I toss a few green leaves in some dressing and bring that to the table. Then, as the timer goes, I take out the pizzas. I divide them with the pizza cutter, slide them onto the plates, and bring them to the table.

"Wow." Arthur watches me sit and pick up a piece. "No knives and forks?"

"If you want, but most people eat pizza with their fingers."

"Excellent." He lifts a piece and bites into it. "Magnificent," he says, his eyes meeting mine.

Is he still talking about the pizza? I'm sure I can see a glimmer of humour in his eyes.

"You overheard me, didn't you?" I say.

He has another bite of the pizza. "Might have."

Heat fills my face. "I'm sorry."

He laughs. "What about?"

"I don't know. I'm embarrassed."

He smiles. "I can see that. You shouldn't be."

"I was asking Immi about her date with Christian, and she mentioned that he kissed her, that's all, and then she asked if we've kissed, and, well, you heard the rest."

He leans on the table and meets my eyes. "You told me you needed time," he says gently.

"I know. I do."

"That's the only reason I haven't kissed you yet."

"Oh. Okay."

"I've thought about it a lot," he says. "Just so you know."

I laugh and poke at an olive on my pizza. "Me too."

"We'll know when it's time," he says. "And until then, I'm enjoying the anticipation."

I look up at him again and lose the power to breathe at the desire in his eyes. He's right. The anticipation is delicious, like making the best chocolate cake you've ever baked, and knowing you're going to have a piece at the end of the day.

"So Christian kissed her," Arthur says, having another bite of pizza. "Glad to hear it."

"She really likes him. She hasn't dated anyone for several years."

"Why not?"

"She went out with a guy when she first became a police officer. His name was Kevin. They lived together for about five years. I really thought they were going to get married, have kids, the whole thing. But one day she came home and found him in bed with someone else."

Arthur stops eating and stares at me. "Seriously?" His eyes are hard. He doesn't approve of that behaviour, thank goodness.

"You know what Immi's like—I thought she would've yelled at him, arrested him, cut up his clothes, thrown him out. But she just turned around and left. She came here and stayed with me and mum for a few weeks, until she found herself another place. At first, she wouldn't talk to me about it. Then one night I came downstairs and found her sitting on the sofa, no lights on, no TV. I asked her if she was all right, and she said no, that she'd found out she was pregnant."

"Oh no."

"Apparently they'd been trying for a baby for a few months. She said she'd had no idea he was unhappy. They were planning the wedding. Hoping to get pregnant. It completely floored her."

"What happened?" Arthur asks softly.

I sigh. "We talked for days about whether she should keep the baby. She was just getting on in her job, and she knew it would be difficult being a single mother. She didn't want that connection with Kevin, not when he'd hurt her so badly. But she said it wasn't the baby's fault that his father was a... well, I won't say what word she used, but it rhymes with 'banker'."

Arthur snorts. "So what did she do?"

"She decided to keep it." I swallow hard at the memory of the tenderness in her eyes when she told me. "And then, a few days later, she had a miscarriage."

Arthur's quiet for a long time. I have another bite of pizza while I wait for him to speak. Then, eventually, I say, "Are you okay?"

He hesitates. "I'm debating whether to tell you something about our previous life together."

I study his face, and for the first time see a glimpse of sorrow behind his eyes. It's not difficult to deduce the meaning. "I had a miscarriage before?" I whisper.

He waits a moment, then gives a reluctant nod. "Several, actually. We never knew why."

I think of how miserable and unhappy Imogen was at the time, and feel a twist inside at the thought that Arthur and Guinevere had gone through the same thing.

"It must be very hard when you love someone and want children with them," I say carefully.

He nods and pokes at his pizza. The memory still stings for him.

"But that was before," I tell him. "That doesn't mean it would happen for you again."

We both know I'm referring to if he were to have children with me. The thought makes my head spin. Physically, even if Guinevere and I look the same, even if we share the same soul, we're not the same person. We can't be. She died. Her body was buried. And mine wouldn't have the same weaknesses as hers. Would it?

He looks up at me. "Do you want children?"

"Yes," I say, without hesitation.

He holds my gaze. "Good," he replies.

My pulse speeds up, and even though we don't speak of it again, and we finish eating our pizzas, my heart continues to race for a long, long time.

Chapter Twenty-One

After we've eaten, we go into the living room and settle down to read for a while with a glass of wine, as Arthur declares he still prefers it to whisky. He sits on the sofa with one of my childhood encyclopaedias and reads slowly through it, occasionally commenting on things he finds interesting.

I curl up in one of the armchairs and pull the chest I found last week of my ancestors' Books of Shadows toward me. I've flicked through most of them, but now I'm taking my time to read them properly, recording any interesting recipes I like in mine, and noting down spells I think I might try.

I pick up one belonging to Harriet—my great-grandmother. It's beautifully decorated—she obviously had a flair for painting, and the front page bears her name, surrounded by colourful flowers. The journal is dated 1939, right before the outbreak of World War II. Harriet would have been eighteen.

Slowly, I turn the pages, enjoying the experience of reconnecting with her as much as reading the information contained inside. Last week, at the hospital when I did a healing spell for Christian's baby niece, I had a vision of my grandmother, who stated that she and Harriet and Josephine all continue to watch over me. I have to trust in them to guide me. Although I believe in free will, I'm a big believer in Fate, and at the moment I very much feel as if I'm being guided down a certain path.

Harriet's journals are a mixture of recipes and spells, and general information about witchcraft interspersed with more local details, like where in Somerset to find particular herbs and crystals. I glance over the intricate paintings of a variety of birds and turn the page.

My heart leaps. Harriet has drawn a triquetra, and beneath it are the letters M and S.

"Arthur!" I get up and run to sit beside him. "Look."

I read out the notes that Harriet wrote on the page opposite the drawing.

"'Today I spoke to my friend Jemima Potter, a local seamstress. I've thought in the past that it's possible she's a witch because of some things she's let slip, and today she admitted she is part of a local coven called Morgana's Sisters, and she invited me to go to one of their regular weekly meetings. I've only ever practiced alone or with my mother, but on Sunday I'm going to go and see what it's like. I'm rather excited!'"

"M and S," I say to Arthur as I turn the page. "Morgana's Sisters."

He nods. "Valerie and her friends were obviously all members of the coven."

I read out the next entry.

"'Today I went to a meeting of Morgana's Sisters. The women were perfectly pleasant. They carried out several rituals and prayers, and had a discussion about the best spell for cleansing negative energy from the home. I had a nice time. But I won't be going back. It's difficult to explain why. They were very secretive, which is their prerogative, of course, but I'm conscious that they didn't tell me everything, and the reason for that made me uncomfortable. I'm a solitary soul, and I'm happy on my own. I don't have to answer to anyone. I have my methods and my spells, and I'm content with exploring new ones on my own.'"

I put the book down. "It's so strange reading this—I feel as if I'm talking directly to my great-grandmother. We seem to have had a lot in common."

"The women in your family were different in some ways and similar in others," Arthur says. "Although you've all got on well with other people, equally you've all been happy on your own."

"I forget that you've seen us all," I say softly. "What was Harriet like?"

"Smaller than you. She had red hair too, and wore it up in a bun, like you do. She was matter-of-fact and practical, quite no-nonsense with Lizzie and her brothers when they were young. She used to sing, like you do." He smiles.

Feeling a little bashful that he watched me for years without me knowing, I look back at the book. "So... Morgana's Sisters. Valerie and her friends must have been very committed to the group to have a tattoo."

"Maybe they'd been together a long time," Arthur suggests.

"Do you think it's possible that *two* of them are murderers?"

Arthur frowns. "We know that Mary did The Star Sign Spell. Harriet said they made her feel uncomfortable. Perhaps they dabble in darker magic. It wouldn't surprise me if she picked up on that."

I read through Harriet's entry again, frowning. Then I get up, retrieve my iPad, and return to the sofa.

"She's got an idea," Arthur says to Merlin.

"I have." I pull up a site called MyFamilyTree.com. "I subscribe to it," I explain to Arthur. "It's for researching your family history, and it gives access to birth, death, and marriage certificates."

I check the name in the journal again, then type "Jemima Potter" into the search box. A list of names comes up, so I refine the search by area, and try again.

"You're looking to see when Jemima was born?" Arthur asks.

"Not quite. I was wondering if Potter was her married name or her maiden name—her surname before she got married." I frown at the screen that still lists numerous Jemima Potters. "Harriet married my great-grandfather in 1943, so if we're assuming Jemima was around the same age as Harriet because they were friends, she might well have married in the forties, too." I refine the search again by the decade. This time, there's only the one page of names.

Arthur and I go through them one by one, clicking on the names and seeing what records exist for them. Eventually, we land on the right one. "Jemima Potter," I say softly, "married Hugh Hopkins in 1941."

"Hopkins," Arthur says. "That can't be a coincidence."

I massage my brow. "Only one way to tell. We'll have to follow the breadcrumbs."

I explain the story of Hansel and Gretel as I find and pull up the birth certificates of Jemima's children. She had four. The eldest had no children of his own. The next had two, a boy and a girl. I check their children's birth certificates—neither of them is called Valerie.

I go back and start again with Jemima's third child. He had four children. Arthur goes to the kitchen and pours us both a glass of wine while I painstakingly search through the certificates. None of them is called Valerie.

Lastly, my heart in my mouth as I wonder whether I'm heading down a dead end, I pull up the details of the fourth child, Ian Hopkins. He had two children. I see their names and inhale sharply.

"There," I exclaim triumphantly, jabbing the screen. Arthur peers over my shoulder. "Jemima's grandchildren. Valerie and Matthew."

"You were right." He smiles at me. "Jemima was related to Valerie."

"I wonder if Matthew discovered this?" I sip my wine thoughtfully. "We know that he hadn't spoken to Valerie for a long time when she died. What if he discovered that Jemima was a witch, and drew the conclusion that Valerie might be too?"

Arthur stretches out his long legs. "If he did, he must have been pretty annoyed that he was descended from one."

"Yes, of course, he would be." I put down the iPad and pick up my wine. "That would be ironic."

"Because he dislikes witches?"

"Yes, but mainly because he's apparently descended from *the* Matthew Hopkins." At Arthur's blank look, I realize he's unaware of that period of English history. "In the seventeenth century," I explain, "there was a civil war in England, and a lot of religious problems between those who wanted the country to stay Catholic, and those who were Puritans and wanted reform. The original Hopkins was a witch-hunter at this time—he gave himself the unofficial title of Witchfinder General. Witches were thought to be heretics to Christianity and were said to have made a covenant with the Devil. It was assumed that the Devil would never confess to his crimes, and therefore a confession had to be forced out of these women. They were tortured and then burned or hanged when they were inevitably found guilty."

Arthur's smile has faded, and his eyes have darkened. "And Matthew is proud of his inheritance?"

"Oh yes. He claims to be channelling the original Hopkins' spirit."

"I dislike the man even more now," Arthur says. "What a..." He purses his lips. "I'm not sure what word to use."

"Idiot?"

"I was thinking of something a little more colourful."

"Plonker?" I giggle. "It's a British-ism."

Arthur grins. "Well back in the sixth century I wouldn't have been so polite, but I'm not amongst soldiers now. Oh, I've just had a thought. You don't think Matthew could have killed his sister?"

My eyebrows rise. "No. Surely not."

"If he is serious about witch hunting, and he's writing books about it, the last thing he'd want would be to have a witch for a sister."

The thought of anyone being a murderer is unpleasant, but the notion of Matthew Hopkins killing his sister makes me very uneasy. "Maybe. I wonder whether Immi has him down as a suspect?"

"I'm sure she does," Arthur says. "It'll be interesting to see if he has an alibi for the morning of the murder. We'll make it our next task to find out. Now, it's time for my history lesson."

I laugh and curl up beside him with my wine. "Fire away."

"Tell me about the English Civil War," he says.

"There have been two," I advise. "One between King Stephen and Matilda in the twelfth century, and one in the seventeenth century."

"Tell me about the seventeenth-century one. I want to know more about religion."

"Well, if you want to know about religion in England, you'd be better off starting with the Reformation."

He nods, so I begin with Henry VIII and the English Reformation, and then move on to the seventeenth-century. The hour grows late, but Arthur is fascinated, and throws question after question at me, making me delve deep to remember the history I've learned over the years.

Eventually, though, I declare I'm going to have to go to bed; I can barely keep my eyes open. "Are you going up?" I ask him, pausing in the doorway.

"I'll stay up a while," he says. "Read a bit more."

"Do you sleep at all?"

"A few hours a night," he says. "I'm hoping that will get better."

"It's still only been three days since you woke up," I reply softly. "It's so hard to believe that. It feels as if you've been here forever."

"Is that a good thing?"

I smile. "Yes. A very good thing."

He smiles back. "I'll see you tomorrow."

"Will you let Merlin out?"

"Yes, of course."

I hesitate for a moment, so tempted to go over to Arthur and kiss him. The look in his eyes suggests he wouldn't be averse to me doing that. But I'm not brave enough. Instead, I go up the stairs.

When I've been to the bathroom, I leave the curtains open, get into bed, and look out at the moon, in its third quarter. My mind feels like a box of bees, buzzing away. I think about Valerie, and swallow hard as I imagine how it must have felt when she fell from the balcony. I want to find her murderer, but I'm not sure if I'm helping Imogen at all. Have I found out anything useful? Something tells me I'm not quite on the right path. I don't know why, but it's a little niggly feeling that something's not right. Lying awake won't solve anything, though.

I turn onto my side and close my eyes. I wish Arthur were here, in bed with me. His body pressed up against mine. His skin would be warm, and I know he'd smell amazing.

As I think about him, the buzzing of the bees quietens, and finally I fall asleep.

Chapter Twenty-Two

The next day, we go to the café in the morning. I bake and serve until the lunchtime rush is over. Cooper takes Arthur to the local DIY store, and they buy several pots of peach-coloured paint for the break room, and a set of rollers and trays. Arthur then spends a couple of hours painting the walls, humming away to the radio playing folk music.

By about two p.m., it's quietening down and we're ready for a break, so I take him on a trip to the supermarket.

He's astounded at the array of food available for purchase and walks up and down the aisles with an open mouth.

"There's so much choice." He picks up two tins of chopped tomatoes, one with garlic, one with Italian herbs, then stares at the other six or seven different options.

"I know; it makes it tough sometimes, having so much to choose from." I always enjoy shopping for ingredients for my baking, but today I especially enjoy his boundless enthusiasm. He's already found it amazing how many fruits and vegetables are available, and his incredulity only increases as he discovers the dried, tinned, and frozen food.

But it's when I take him to the bread aisle that I find myself truly humbled. He walks slowly through the tables of baked goods and the cabinets of fresh breads, occasionally picking up a packet of rolls or a loaf. When he gets to the end, he turns to me, and I'm shocked to see him genuinely choked up.

"Hey." I slip my arm beneath his and walk him to a quiet corner of the aisle. "What's up?"

"I'm sorry." He gives a short laugh and runs his hand through his hair. "It's just... not long before my last battle, there was bad weather, and the crops failed. Everyone went hungry, and there was widespread famine. I look at all this food, all this bread, and it makes me think about my soldiers, and how much they suffered…" He stops speaking, fighting against emotion.

"I'm so sorry." I rub his arm, keeping my voice light and practical, to give him time to recover. "I'd read that there was a famine in the year 536—that must be the one you're referring to. Archaeologists think a volcanic eruption threw dust into the atmosphere which affected the weather. They've found evidence that supports it in the growth of tree rings in Ireland."

"Really?" He lets out a long breath, meets my eyes, and smiles. "I might have known you'd understand."

"I've read a lot about the Dark Ages," I say. "I've always found it fascinating. Now I know why."

He lifts a hand and cups my face, taking my breath away. "I thought you were the woman I married," he murmurs, "but you're not."

I blink at him. "What do you mean? You don't think I'm Guinevere anymore?"

"No, not that. You are she. Beautiful, intelligent, practical, fierce when you have to be. But you're much more compassionate. Thoughtful." He strokes my cheek. "Amazing."

His gaze drops to my lips. He's going to kiss me—right here. When Immi asks me *Where did he kiss you?* I'll have to say in the bread aisle of the supermarket. The thought makes a nervous giggle form in my chest that wants to rise, but I hold it in as he moves closer, my heart pounding, barely breathing…

Someone standing a few feet away clears their throat, and Arthur drops his hand. I step back and look at the man who's holding a basket filled with an odd mixture of bread, eggs, peanut butter, and chocolate bars. I recognize him, but I'm so flustered I can't place him for a moment. He's in his forties, and his grey hair looks ruffled, as if he hasn't brushed it. He's wearing an old tracksuit, and there's a stain on the front.

"I'm sorry," he says. "It's just… you're Gwen, aren't you?"

"That's right." I try to focus on him. "I'm sorry, I can't place you," I admit.

"I'm Bradley Brown. Valerie's husband."

The penny drops, and I feel a wave of sorrow for this poor man. "Oh, Bradley, how are you doing?" Immediately, I flush. "That's a stupid question, I'm so sorry."

A ghost of a smile appears on his lips. "It's okay. It's nice to talk to someone. You'd be surprised how many people have avoided me. They've literally crossed the road so they don't have to talk to me." He moves the basket from one hand to another and looks aimlessly around the store. "Kianna said she'd do the shopping, but I needed to get out the house, do something normal. Then I got here and realized I don't have a clue what to buy."

"Can I help?" I ask gently.

His gaze comes back to me, and he shakes his head. "No, no, it's all right. I'll manage. I know we don't know each other, but I understand that you are the one who found Valerie, and I just wanted to say thank you, you know, for calling the police and everything."

"Oh. Well, I only did what anyone would do."

"I don't know. Maybe. But thank you anyway. I don't really know what I'm doing," he admits. "It's strange how the brain works. I've lost the ability to think straight."

"Don't be too hard on yourself." I touch his upper arm. "You've had a terrible shock."

He nods and swallows hard. "The police told me they think she died under suspicious circumstances."

I glance at Arthur, who gives me a pitying look. "Yes, I heard," I say softly. "I'm so sorry."

"I can't imagine who'd want to hurt Valerie," Bradley says. "I mean, she could be a bit in your face at times, and she wasn't afraid to say what she thought, but I don't know that anyone hated her."

I fight with myself as to whether I should use this opportunity to question him. I don't want to distress him; equally, I doubt I'll get another chance.

"I can't imagine either," I reply. "Does her brother have any ideas?"

Bradley's face immediately hardens. "Matthew and I are not on speaking terms."

I pretend to be embarrassed, which isn't far from the truth. "Oh no, I'm sorry, I didn't realize. Now I've put my foot in it."

"It's okay," he says, "you weren't to know. He and Valerie had a big argument several years ago, and he was very mean to her."

"That doesn't surprise me," I can't help adding.

Bradley gives a wry smile. "Yeah, I don't think many people can stomach him."

"Do you know what they argued about?" It's an invasive question and I don't like asking it, but luckily Bradley just nods.

"It was after he started doing that research for his book," he says, surprising me.

"The one about witchcraft in Somerset?"

"Yes. He discovered that two witches were hanged near Glastonbury," he says.

"I know; one of them was my ancestor," I tell him, "Alice Young. She had the same name as my mother."

Bradley's eyebrows rise. "How strange. Because Valerie had done some family research ages ago, you know, for the kids, and she told him that they're both related to the other one—Elizabeth Burrows."

Arthur and I stare at him. "Oh my," I whisper. "No wonder he's mad."

"Yeah." Bradley snorts. "Talk about a hypocrite. Calls himself the Witchfinder General reborn, and then finds out he's related to a witch. He wasn't happy about that, I can tell you. He insisted Valerie was wrong, and when she refused to back down, he demanded she never tell anyone. He was right in her face—I had to step in and intercede. He walked out, and they never spoke again, to my knowledge."

"How awful." I don't have to act distressed. I've experienced Matthew's fury first-hand, so I know how it feels. "Has he been around since she died?"

"He called in yesterday, actually," Bradley says. "He wanted to know if he could have all her family research. I told him to…" He glances at Arthur, then back at me. "Sod off," he finishes lamely. "Luckily, he said he had an appointment and he had to go."

"How insensitive of him; that must have been distressing for you."

"It was." He looks away, out through the supermarket windows at the sunny afternoon. "It should be raining," he murmurs, almost inaudibly. "There should be thunder and lightning. Not sunshine. It doesn't make sense."

His eyes are haunted as he obviously recalls some memory of his late wife. Without another word to us, he turns and wanders off toward the checkouts.

I look up at Arthur, who's frowning. "So that was why Matthew looked upset when we saw him," I say quietly. "Well that's a strange twist."

"He did look angry," Arthur says. "Angry enough to murder her?"

"I wouldn't put it past him," I reply. "He's a horrible man."

"He must be, for you to say so." He's carrying the basket, and he takes my hand in his free one. "Come on. Let's go."

We pay for our goods, go back to the car, and return home, fussing Merlin up when we go in.

"I'm going to ring Immi," I tell Arthur as he puts items in the fridge.

"Okay. I'll make us a coffee."

Smiling, I dial Imogen's number and sit at the pine table. She answers after a couple of rings.

"DCI Hobbs." She sounds as if she's on speakerphone. I can hear an engine, too; she's in the car.

"It's me," I say. "Are you busy?"

"I'm on my way to an interview," she says. "I've got a few minutes."

"I've just seen Bradley Brown in the supermarket," I tell her. "He told me something very interesting." I explain Bradley's revelation about Matthew Hopkins.

"Oh…" She draws the word out. "That is interesting."

"I thought you'd like to know."

"Yes, absolutely. I'm going to see Matthew now," she says.

"Oh, well, that was good timing."

"Mmm. He rang me. Said he has some information."

I sit up. "Oh? You think he's involved?

"Indirectly, maybe." Her phone beeps. "Sorry," she says, "I've got another call coming in. I'll call you back later."

"Of course, 'bye." I hang up, frustrated that she wasn't able to give me more information. Still, she doesn't like sharing details of any case she's working on, so she might not have told me anyway.

Arthur brings over a coffee. "What did she say?"

"Thank you. She said Matthew rang her and announced that he had some information about the case. She said he might be involved indirectly."

"Oh, interesting." He gives Merlin a biscuit from the dog tin on the shelf, brings the human cookies over, then sits opposite me and opens the tin. "Ooh. Chocolate."

I smile and watch him dunk a cookie in his coffee. "It didn't take you long to pick up that technique."

"I'm a fast learner. So I wonder what Immi meant about Matthew having information about the case?" He crunches the cookie thoughtfully. "Do you think he knows who did it? How would he have worked it out?"

I sigh. "I don't know. I still don't think any of the possible suspects has a strong motive." I sip my coffee. "Who do we know had an issue with Valerie? There are her friends, Fenella, Nancy, and Leah."

"Bradley's sister, Kianna?"

"Maybe, although I don't know what her motive would be. Fenella had the argument with Valerie about her dog being poisoned. Nancy was up against her for the promotion in the Living History group. Leah was running against her for the school board. But are any of those strong enough motives for murder?"

"Hmm. What's our next step?"

"I don't know." I sit back in my chair and look out at the garden. It's clouding over, and a few spots of rain land on the window. "Maybe we'll have a read for a while, what do you think?"

"I'm always happy to do that."

So we go into the living room, get the fire going, and I curl up on the sofa, while Arthur stretches out his long legs in the armchair, still working his way through the encyclopaedia.

I pull the box of journals toward me and hover my hand over them. Merlin comes over and snuffles around in the box.

"There's no food in there," I scold. "The dust will get up your nose."

Sure enough, he sneezes, but he doesn't stop snuffling. Before I can push him away, he closes his jaws around one of the journals, gently pulls it out, and lies it on the carpet in front of me.

I stare at it. "What's so special about this one?" I look up at Arthur.

His gaze drops to the dog, then back to me. "He doesn't know. He said he has a hunch."

"All right." I pick it up and settle back. "I'd better find out why."

Chapter Twenty-Three

The journal turns out to be Josephine's—my great-great-grandmother's.

I've already read this one, but I leaf through it again slowly, taking time to note the sketches of plants and herbs, and reading through the spells.

"Anything yet?" Arthur says about ten minutes later, putting down the encyclopaedia.

"Nothing's jumping out at me." I read through a passage on crystal energy and turn the page. "Maybe there's nothing in here that…" My voice trails off.

Arthur gets up and comes to sit beside me on the sofa. Josephine has written a page on poisonous plants in England.

I count them up. "She's listed seventeen."

"How many of these did you know about?" he asks.

"Some. Foxgloves, obviously. Water hemlock. Belladonna. Monkshood. I didn't know that the daffodil was poisonous. Or the hydrangea."

I read out Josephine's next paragraph. "The ingestion of even one flower or leaf from some of these plants can be deadly. But also be careful about burning them, as inhaling the smoke could prove a problem. There are also reports of people falling ill from honey made from bees who have visited some of these flowers."

I look up at Arthur, and we stare at each other for a long time.

"Nancy keeps bees," he says. "But there were no foxgloves in her garden."

"No." My brain is working furiously. I scan the list of plants again. "She had oleander, though."

Arthur thinks about it. "But Immi told you that the coroner said Valerie was poisoned with digoxin."

"Actually, no, she didn't. She'd forgotten the name, and when I suggested it, she said yes. Digoxin is something called a cardiac glycoside, and I'm sure it's in foxgloves." I pick up my iPad and start typing.

After a minute or two, I find what I'm looking for. I exclaim and turn it to show Arthur. "I was right; digoxin is in foxgloves. Oleander contains another cardiac glucoside called digitoxigenin." I indicate the line on the page. "'The clinical effects of oleander poisoning are similar to Digoxin toxicity.' Immi would have read that on the coroner's report and must have remembered the name when I said it."

"An easy mistake to make," Arthur comments. "So let's assume the substance that Valerie was poisoned with came from the oleander in Nancy's garden. Do you think she purposely poisoned Valerie? Or do you think the bees fed on the oleander flowers, and the honey was poisoned by mistake?"

"I don't know." I frown. "We know that Nancy desperately wanted the promotion to team leader of the Living History group, but that doesn't seem like a strong enough motive for murder."

"True. But we mustn't forget the presence of your watch at the site," Arthur says. "It implies someone pushed Valerie, or at least that someone else was there when she died, and they tried to implicate you."

Frustration bubbles up inside me. "Why would Nancy do that? I don't know her well."

"She's probably jealous of you," Arthur says.

"Why?" I ask, puzzled.

He gives me a look that says, *Honestly, woman.* "Because you're beautiful and smart and popular."

"Popular? I've never been popular."

"You're not at school now," he says patiently. "You're well liked in the community, Gwen. People trust your opinion and come to you for advice."

He's right; my opinion of myself stems from school, where I had bright ginger hair, sticky-out teeth, and glasses. I look different now, but inside I'll always be that shy, plain child who nobody wanted to play with.

"I'll ring Immi and tell her what we've found out," I say.

"Good idea."

I dial Imogen's number, but for once it goes to the answerphone. "She must be busy." I hang up and send her an email instead. *Immi— can you double-check the name of the poison that killed Valerie? Digitoxigenin comes from the oleander plant. Honey made from bees who feed on the flowers is also poisonous. Didn't you say she had honey for breakfast? Maybe to sweeten her tea? Nancy has oleander flowers in her garden. Might be worth investigating.*

I press send and put down my iPad. I feel edgy and frustrated. I get up and pick up my coffee cup to take it out to the kitchen. I happen to glance at the crystal ball on top of the mantlepiece, and the cup rattles in the saucer as I see a face looking back at me that isn't mine.

"What is it?" Arthur says, getting to his feet.

"I saw Valerie's face." I rub the edge of my sleeve on the sphere. "It's gone now." My heart's racing, though. "Is she trying to tell me something? Why does she keep appearing?"

Arthur gently takes the cup from my hand. "Shall we take Merlin for a walk? Stretch our legs?"

I swallow and nod. He understands that I need to do something. I can't just sit here and wait for Imogen to call. "Okay."

We don our jackets and shoes and head out into the blustery spring afternoon, Merlin at our heels.

"Let's go into town," I tell him. "I'll pick up another bottle of wine for tonight."

"All right."

The occasional drop of rain touches my face and the wind whips my hair, but it's refreshing. I'm not a police officer; I can't bring Nancy in for questioning. I've passed on the information, and now I have to wait for Imogen to do her bit.

It's getting late, and some of the shops are starting to close. As we approach Mackenzie's Jewellery Shop, I see James in the process of locking the shutters before he goes home.

"Hi James," I say, stopping before him.

He looks around and beams. "Hello, you two. You've chosen a gusty afternoon for a walk."

"Needed to get rid of the cobwebs," I tell him. "How are you?"

"I'm fine." He finishes fastening the padlock and turns to me. Then he hesitates. "How's your detective work going?" he asks.

My eyebrows rise. "What do you mean?"

He gives me a small smile. "Imogen came into the shop a few days ago to get a new battery for her watch. She told me how you helped her solve Liza's murder. And I know you well enough to know that when you questioned Nancy the other day, you weren't just being polite."

I laugh. "You've got me there. I have been trying to help where I can."

His smile fades, and he glances behind him, as if making sure he isn't being overheard.

"Everything all right, James?" Arthur asks.

James's gaze comes back to us. "I've just discovered something odd, and I don't know whether it's important."

My heart skips a beat. "Oh?"

He clears his throat, then obviously decides he might as well tell us what's bothered him. "On Tuesday, I opened up the shop at eight thirty, then when Nancy turned up at nine, I asked her to hold the fort while I nipped out to the post office."

"Hold the fort?" Arthur says.

"It means to look after the place while you're away," I explain.

"Ah."

"I went out around nine," James says. "For about thirty minutes. When I came back, Nancy was there, cleaning the clocks. But I've just bumped into one of my customers. She lives out of town and works in one of the cafés here on Tuesdays and Fridays. She jokingly asked if I overslept on Tuesday, because she came in early to pick up a ring she'd had altered, and the shop was shut."

"Just after nine o'clock?" Arthur says. "That's when Valerie died."

"I know," James says. He studies his shoes for a moment. "I feel bad for telling you. Nancy's worked for me for a long time, and she's diligent and hardworking. But lately…" He gives a long sigh.

"Has something changed?" I ask softly.

"She started seeing someone a few months ago," he says. "I think she's in love with him. And it's making her a bit…" He pauses. Then he rotates his forefinger around his ear.

"Crazy?" I ask.

"Mm," James says. "I don't think he's serious about her. But you know what it's like when you're in love. You'd do anything for that person."

I don't look at Arthur, but my face warms.

"Do you know who it is that she's seeing?" I ask James.

"Of course," James says. "It's Matthew Hopkins."

And, like one of those puzzles with the little square tiles that slide around to make a picture, everything slots into place.

Arthur looks across at me and goes still. "Gwen…" He looks at James. "She's had a Europa moment."

"Eureka," I correct. "But yes, I have. Where is Nancy now?" I ask James urgently. "Has she gone home?"

"She was working at the abbey this afternoon," James says. "They're short-staffed because Valerie's not there."

"Thank you." I reach up and kiss him on the cheek. Then I say to Arthur, "come on, we need to catch her before she goes."

I wave goodbye to James and run across the road. Arthur and Merlin catch up with me as I stride back up the high street to the market cross and turn into Magdalene Street, toward the Avalon Café.

"So Nancy's having an affair with Matthew," Arthur states, his long legs easily keeping up with me.

"It all makes sense now," I reply. We cross the road and enter the abbey shop. Oscar waves us through, and we exit onto the lawn, with the Lady Chapel in front of us. The police have removed the tape they originally set up around the scene, and a small group of tourists is making their way through the chapel, led by a woman in a long blue medieval gown.

"Nancy." I stop at the edge of the chapel. I don't know what I'm going to say to her yet, just that I have to talk to her.

She turns and sees us, and her voice trails off. Her eyes meet mine, and we study each other for a long time.

Finally, she looks back at the tourists with a smile and says, "You must excuse me for a moment. Please continue on to the nave, and take a look at the site of Arthur's tomb."

Arthur shivers beside me, but I don't have time to console him, because Nancy's walking toward us.

She stops on the grass before us, then looks away, across to where we found Valerie just a few days ago.

Chapter Twenty-Four

"Yes?" Nancy asks. Her tone is polite, but her eyes are icy.

"Sorry to bother you," I reply. "I'd just like to ask you a quick question. On Tuesday morning—around nine a.m., when Valerie died—I understand that you left the jewellery shop. Can you tell me where you went?"

A touch of colour appears in her cheeks. "That's private," she says. "Anyway, what's it got to do with you?"

"I'm clearing something up for DCI Hobbs," I say. "It's an easy question."

For a moment she doesn't reply. I can see her weighing up whether to refuse to answer, or whether she thinks that will look more suspicious. Beside me, Arthur folds his arms, and Merlin sits, all of us waiting patiently for her reply.

Eventually, she snaps, "I was with my boyfriend. I popped out of the shop to see him."

I meet her eyes. "I think you should know that Matthew called Imogen earlier, and she went around to interview him. So you'd better be sure of your story."

Her jaw drops. "You're lying," she whispers.

"I'm not. I understand why you fell for him. Matthew is good-looking, intelligent, and charismatic." I frown. "But I am surprised you continued to be interested in him once you discovered his dislike for witches."

As soon as I say that, Nancy's defences crumble. Her shoulders sag, and tears well in her eyes.

"You poisoned Valerie with the oleander honey because she told you to stop seeing her brother," I accuse. "You thought Matthew would be pleased because you thought he hated her, but you underestimated his love for his sister. I think he was coming to see you when we met you at your house yesterday. I think you told him what you'd done, and he was so angry that he broke up with you. He must have thought about what you'd done all night, and today he decided he couldn't keep it a secret, and he rang Imogen."

Nancy looks away, a bit vague, as if she's only half with me. "Valerie hated that I was going out with him. She saw it as a betrayal of Morgana's Sisters, and told me that if I didn't stop seeing him, she'd tell him the truth about me being a witch."

"I presume you knew that the honey you gave Valerie was poisonous?" Arthur asks. "And if so, if you knew it would probably kill her, why did you push her over the barrier at the abbey?"

"I got an email from the Living History team to say that I hadn't got the promotion." Her cheeks redden, and her jaw knots. "And then she sent me a smug text to say she'd got it. I was furious. I had to see her. I'd given her the honey, because she'd told me she has it in her tea every day, but even though she was sick, it was taking too long. When I saw her in the Lady Chapel, I didn't stop to think. I just pushed her over the edge."

She looks past me and sighs. I turn and follow her gaze and see Imogen running across the lawn toward us, two police officers hot on her heels. I turn back to Nancy.

"Why did you leave my watch at the scene?" I whisper. "You obviously meant to frame me for Valerie's murder. Why?"

"It was your fault that Mary is in prison," she says fiercely. "Imogen told us that you helped her catch her. You're so perfect. Sticking your nose in where it doesn't belong. Even Matthew thinks you're the bee's knees. I hate you." Her eyes blaze with sudden hatred, making me catch my breath.

"Hello, hello." Imogen stops before us all, panting a little. "What's going on here, then?"

"Nancy has just confessed to murdering Valerie," Arthur states.

"I see." Imogen beckons to the officer who arrives beside her, takes a pair of handcuffs from him, and walks up to Nancy. "Nancy Armstrong, I'm arresting you for the murder of Valerie Hopkins-Brown," she states. "You do not have to say anything, but it may harm your defence if you do not mention..." She continues reading Nancy her rights as she cuffs both Nancy's wrists behind her back.

When she's done, Imogen meets my gaze and raises an eyebrow. "Beat me to it again, huh?"

"Sorry."

She smiles. "Don't apologize. You'll come in to give a statement tomorrow morning? Tell me everything you found out?"

"Of course."

"How did you know?" Nancy asks Imogen. "Did she tell you?"

"Nope," Imogen replies. "Your boyfriend threw you under the bus, I'm afraid. I wouldn't go so far as to say he's one of the good guys, but he wasn't going to keep the information about his sister's death quiet. Now come on. I'd like to get home before midnight tonight. Let's get a move on." She marches Nancy away over the lawn toward the waiting police car.

"Under the bus?" Arthur says.

"It means to betray someone selfishly," I advise. "Idioms are one of the hardest things to understand when learning a language."

He smiles and puts his arms around my shoulders. "Are you okay? I have a feeling that what Nancy said upset you."

"It's rare that someone says they hate me," I reply.

"As I said, she was jealous and angry," Arthur tells me. "Try not to take it to heart." He squeezes my shoulders. "Shall we go home?"

"Actually, I have one thing I'd like to do first," I tell him. "Would you take Merlin home for me? I won't be long."

"Are you sure you'll be okay?"

I take a deep breath and blow it out slowly. "I'm fine."

"Then of course." He doesn't question me, just kisses my temple, then clicks his fingers at Merlin, and heads off home.

I watch him go, my stomach fluttering with several different emotions.

Turning, I walk slowly back across the lawn. What a couple of weeks it's been. I'm pleased to have found Valerie's murderer, but upset as well at the thought of everything that's happened. Nancy's hatred shocked me, as did her declaration that Matthew thinks I'm the "bee's knees." I knew he liked me, but her words made me feel very uncomfortable.

There's been a lot of negative energy flowing around lately, and I want to do something positive. Something I've been meaning to do for a while.

I walk around to the museum entrance, push open the doors, and go inside.

*

I get home about thirty minutes later.

149

"That didn't take long." Arthur looks up from where he's sitting on the sofa, Merlin at his feet.

"Just calling in a favour," I tell him. "I'll explain more tomorrow."

"Okay." He smiles.

"Aren't you going to ask what it is?" I say playfully.

"You'll tell me when you're ready."

I smile. "You're a good man, Arthur."

"Not all the time." He gives me a lazy smile that sends a shiver down my spine.

"Oh. I—" My reply is cut short as Merlin barks, something he does very rarely. I look around, puzzled, then inhale sharply as I look at Mum's old decorative mirror above the sofa. Valerie is standing behind me, dressed in white, her hair floating around her shoulders as if in a small breeze.

Arthur gets to his feet and stands by my side, looking at the mirror.

"Can you see her?" I whisper.

He nods. "It's time," he replies. "She's ready to move on, now."

Merlin walks up and sits beside him. Arthur holds my hand.

For a moment, there's just the ticking of the clock on the wall and the crackling of the logs in the grate. I'm conscious of Arthur's chest rising and falling with each breath. His fingers tighten.

Before us, a ball of light forms. It's about the size of the crystal ball on the mantlepiece. It's so bright, I can barely look at it.

It's the Grail—the well of energy.

Threads of light emerge from the ball and reach toward us. I feel them enter my body, filling me with warmth and love. I feel as if I'm glowing, too, but when I look up, the threads have passed through us and have engulfed Valerie's spirit in a ball of white light. It glows brighter and brighter; I close my eyes, it's so bright.

When I open them again, the Grail has gone, and so has Valerie.

I look up at Arthur. He smiles. "She's at peace now," he says.

And, for the first time in several days, so am I.

*

The next morning, Arthur and I go to the station to see Imogen and give our statement detailing all the information we found out about Nancy and the oleander honey. When we're done, we go back to the café, and Arthur finishes painting the break room, while I spend the morning baking.

It's around one p.m. that I hear a commotion in the café, with a couple of people cheering and clapping. I look up through the window that separates it from the kitchen and grin as I see what's happening. Wiping my hands on a tea towel, I go out into the café, where Nathan, who's the head of the Arthurian Adventure, and Christian, are in the process of moving Sir Boss back to his spot by the café door.

"Thank you so much," I say, oddly tearful to have the knight back where he belongs.

"Shouldn't have been moved in the first place," Nathan says gruffly. He's a big guy in his forties with a brown beard flecked with grey. "It took a couple of phone calls, but eventually the Health and Safety Department at the council agreed we could move him back, providing he was properly restrained." The knight's raised hand is chained to the upper part of the suit so the sword can't fall.

"That's wonderful," I say. "Perfect."

"And here's the other thing you asked for." Nathan holds out a small box.

I take it from him. "Thank you."

"This is rather unusual," Nathan says, "but I think we know you well enough to be sure you're not going to sell it or lose it."

"I think it will be taken very good care of," Christian adds.

Feeling a wave of emotion, I just nod, and the two men smile and wave as they leave the café.

Turning, I see Arthur coming through the door of the break room, presumably to see what all the fuss is about. He stops as he sees Sir Boss, then laughs and strides up to the suit of armour. "That's good to see." He reaches out a hand to brush a fleck of dirt off the knight's breastplate.

"It didn't seem right, him not being here," I tell him. Then I slip my hand into his. "Come with me," I whisper.

I lead him outside, into the afternoon sunshine. The rainclouds left this morning, and now it's a beautiful day, the stones of the abbey turned golden in the sun.

"What's this about?" Arthur raises an eyebrow as I turn him to face me.

"I have a present for you." I hold out the box.

"It's not my birthday," he says, taking it.

"I know. I just wanted to say thank you for your help in solving the case, and… well…" I feel suddenly shy. "I wanted to let you know that I'm glad you're here."

He meets my eyes for a moment. His are very blue—the colour of the sky behind his head. Then he drops his gaze to the box and pulls off the lid.

It's the bronze brooch in the shape of a bear that I gave to him in my previous incarnation for our fifth wedding anniversary.

He stares at it, then lifts it out of the box. "How did you get it?" he whispers.

"I asked Nathan if I could look after it. He knows how much I love archaeology, so he said yes."

Arthur rubs a thumb over the bear, obviously fighting against a rise of emotion. "You did this for me?"

"I don't want you to think that because I don't remember our past, you're not very special to me."

He lowers his hand and meets my eyes. To my right is the abbey, which bears our graves in the centre of the nave. To our left is the café, through which I know we're being watched by Delia, Melissa, and Cooper, as well as a dozen customers.

But Arthur seems oblivious to everything as he lifts his free hand and slides it to the back of my neck. He moves closer, and puts his other arm around me, still holding the box.

I rest my hand on his chest and hold my breath, my heart hammering against my ribs at the affection, the desire, in his eyes.

And then he lowers his lips to mine.

I close my eyes, sighing as he kisses me. Everything flees my mind. There's only Arthur's firm lips, the scent of his new aftershave, the feel of his muscles through his sweater beneath my fingers, the touch of the sun slanting across us, warm on my face. Merlin sits by our feet, and I'm sure he's smiling. It feels as if I've come home.

The sound of cheering from the café makes us laugh and break apart. I wave to everyone inside, then slide my arms around Arthur's waist and lean my cheek on his chest, looking out across the grounds of the abbey.

"Summer's on its way," I murmur, and Arthur kisses the top of my head.

A Knight to Remember (The Avalon Café Book 3)

He's one knight she'll never forget…

When kitchen witch Gwen Young discovers a local artist has gone missing, she and Arthur set out to solve the mystery. Neither of them suspects that their past – and their future – is closely tied to this case…

Now available on Amazon!

*

Join the Avalon Café Readers!

Want to know when the next Avalon Café story is available? Join my mailing list to stay informed, and you'll also be able to download a free, exclusive short story (not for sale) about how Gwen met Merlin! Go to my website for more details:

Website: http://www.hermionemoon.com

About the Author

Hermione Moon writes cozy witch mysteries with a sprinkling of romance, set in Glastonbury, England. She also writes steamy contemporary romance as Serenity Woods, and is a USA Today bestselling author under that name. She currently lives with her husband in New Zealand.

Website: http://www.hermionemoon.com

Facebook: https://www.facebook.com/hermionemoonauthor

Made in the USA
Coppell, TX
25 June 2020